Doomed Love

VIRGIL

Doomed Love

Translated by W. F. JACKSON KNIGHT

GREAT 🐧🐧 LOVES

To T. J. Haarhoff

PENGUIN BOOKS

Published by the Penguin Group
Penguin Books Ltd, 80 Strand, London WC2R ORL, England
Penguin Group (USA) Inc., 375 Hudson Street, New York, New York 10014, USA
Penguin Group (Canada), 90 Eglinton Avenue East, Suite 700, Toronto, Ontario, Canada M4P 2Y3
(a division of Pearson Penguin Canada Inc.)
Penguin Ireland, 25 St Stephen's Green, Dublin 2, Ireland
(a division of Penguin Books Ltd)
Penguin Group (Australia), 250 Camberwell Road, Camberwell, Victoria 3124, Australia
(a division of Pearson Australia Group Pty Ltd)
Penguin Books India Pvt Ltd, 11 Community Centre, Panchsheel Park, New Delhi – 110 017, India
Penguin Group (NZ), 67 Apollo Drive, Rosedale, North Shore 0632, New Zealand
(a division of Pearson New Zealand Ltd)
Penguin Books (South Africa) (Pty) Ltd, 24 Sturdee Avenue,
Rosebank, Johannesburg 2196, South Africa

Penguin Books Ltd, Registered Offices: 80 Strand, London WC2R ORL, England

www.penguin.com

This translation of the *Aneneid* first published 1956
Reprinted with revisions 1958
This extract published in Penguin Books 2007

2

Copyright © G. R. Wilson Knight 1956, 1958
All rights reserved

Typeset by Rowland Phototypesetting Ltd, Bury St Edmunds, Suffolk
Printed in England by Clays Ltd, St Ives plc

978-0-141-03478-2

Contents

Publius Vergilius Maro (70 B.C. to 19 B.C.), known as Virgil, was born near Mantua in the last days of the Roman Republic. In his comparatively short life he became the supreme poet of his age, whose major work, the *Aeneid*, gave Rome a great national epic equal to the Greeks', celebrating the city's origins and the creation of its empire. The first four books of the epic, selected for this edition, tell how the Trojan hero Aeneas escapes from the sacking of Troy and makes his way to Italy. On the voyage, a storm drives him to the coast of Carthage, where the queen, Dido, welcomes him, and under the influence of the gods falls deeply in love with him.

BOOK ONE
Of Gods and Angry Seas

I am that poet who in times past made the light
melody of pastoral poetry. In my next poem I left the
woods for the adjacent farmlands, teaching them to
obey even the most exacting tillers of the soil; and
the farmers liked my work. But now I turn to the
terrible strife of Mars.

This is a tale of arms and of a man. Fated to be an
exile, he was the first to sail from the land of Troy
and reach Italy, at its Lavinian shore. He met many
tribulations on his way both by land and on the ocean;
high Heaven willed it, for Juno was ruthless and could
not forget her anger. And he had also to endure great
suffering in warfare. But at last he succeeded in
founding his city, and installing the gods of his race in
the Latin land: and that was the origin of the Latin
nation, the Lords of Alba, and the proud battlements
of Rome.

I pray for inspiration, to tell how it all began, and
how the Queen of Heaven sustained such outrage to
her majesty that in her indignation she forced a man
famed for his true-heartedness to tread that long path

of adventure, and to face so many trials. It is hard to believe Gods in Heaven capable of such rancour.

Once there was an ancient town called Carthage, inhabited by emigrants from Tyre, and confronting Italy, opposite to the mouth of the Tiber but far away. Carthage had wealth and power; and it had skill and ferocity in war. Now Juno is said to have loved Carthage best of all cities in the world, giving even Samos the second place. She kept her weapons and her chariot there; and she had already set her heart on making it a capital city governing all the earth, and spared no effort of fostering care, hoping that Destiny might consent to her desire. She had, however, heard of another breed of men, tracing descent from the blood of Troy, who were one day to overthrow this Tyrian stronghold: for they would breed a warrior nation, haughty, and sovereign over wide realms; and their onset would bring destruction to Africa. Such, she had heard, was the plan of the spinning Fates, and it was this plan that Juno feared. Neither could she forget the Trojan War, when she had battled in the forefront for the Argos which she loved. She remembered the origin of that quarrel and the fierce indignation which it had caused her. The judgement of Paris, with its unjust slight to her beauty, remained indelibly stamped on her mind; and besides she was always jealous of the whole Trojan race, and could not forget how Ganymede had been stolen and honoured.

Such were the causes of Juno's fury. And so it was that the Trojan remnant, whom the Greeks, even pitiless Achilles, could not kill, were tossed in storm over all the ocean; and still she kept them far from Latium, wandering for years at the mercy of fate from sea to sea about the world. Such was the cost in heavy toil of beginning the life of Rome.

The Trojans had put out to sea from Sicily. They were just out of sight of land, the bronze-plated oars churning the salt water to foam, and they were happily hoisting sail when Juno, perpetually nursing her heart's deep wound, spoke to herself:

'I, vanquished? I, to abandon the fight? Lacking even the strength to keep Troy's prince from making Italy? The Fates forbid me, indeed! Yet they never stopped Minerva from gutting the Argives' fleet by fire, and drowning all of them, merely because one man, Ajax son of Oileus, he alone, went mad, and sinned. She borrowed Jupiter's devouring fire, and sped it from the clouds. She shattered the ships, and tore up the surface of ocean with winds. And when Ajax, pierced through the breast by the lightning-flame, was breathing his last, she caught him up in a tornado and impaled him on a pointed rock. Yet I, in my stately precedence, Queen of all the Divine, I, the sister and wife of Jove, have been making war for all these years on a single clan. Will anyone again pay reverence to Juno's majesty, or lay his offering on her altar in humble prayer?'

Debating so with herself in her fiery brain, she went straight to Aeolia where the storm-clouds have their home and mad winds are bursting to be free. In the great spaces of a cavern they wrestle, and hurricaness roar: but Aeolus, the king who rules them, confines them in their prison, disciplined and curbed. They race from door to bolted door, and all the mountain reverberates with the noise of their resentment. But Aeolus, throned securely above them, sceptre in hand, tempers their arrogance and controls their fury. Otherwise they would sweep violently away with them every land, every sea, and the very depths of the sky, and drive them all through space. Foreseeing this, therefore, the Father with whom is all power banished the winds to that dark cavern, and piled above them a mountain mass, appointing a king over them who, under a fixed charter, would know how to hold them confined and also, when so commanded, to give them a free rein. To this King of the Winds Juno now made her submissive appeal.

'To you, my Lord Aeolus, he who is father of all gods and king of all men has given authority to lull the waves or to rouse them with a wind. Now a certain people whom I hate are sailing on the Etruscan Sea, and conveying Troy itself and the vanquished gods of Trojan homes to Italy. Smite fury into your winds. Sink their ships; make the sea close over them. Or drive them apart, pitch out their crews, and scatter them on the deep. I chance to have fourteen sea-nymphs of striking beauty, and Deiopea is the loveliest of them all. I shall assign her to be yours in lawful marriage, and in return for your great goodness to me she shall live out with you all the years to come and make you father of splendid sons.'

Replying, Aeolus spoke thus: 'Highness, your sole task is to decide what your wish is to be; and my only duty is prompt obedience to you. I owe to you all my authority in this little realm of mine, for it was you who won for me Jupiter's favour. I owe to you my place at the feasts of the Immortals; and from you I hold my power over storm-clouds and over storms.'

This said, he swung his trident round where the shell of the cliff was thin, and struck home. The winds formed line, and charged through the outlet which he had made. With tornado blasts they swept the earth. They swooped down on the sea. Winds of the east and the south, and the African Wind with squall after squall, came tearing from their depths, and set the long rollers rolling to the shores. Now men were shouting and tackle shrieking. In a moment the clouds had wrested from Trojan eyes the sky and the light of day: a blackness as of night fell on the ocean. The thunder cracked in heaven's height, and in the air above a continuous lightning flared; wherever the Trojans looked, immediate death stared them in the eyes. Instantly Aeneas felt his limbs give way in a chill of terror, and groaned. Stretching both hands, palm-upward, to the stars, he cried aloud: 'How fortunate were you, thrice fortunate and more, whose luck it was to die under the high walls of Troy before your parents' eyes! Ah, Diomede, most valiant of Greeks, why did your arm not strike me down and give my spirit freedom in death on the battlefields of Ilium, where lie the mighty Sarpedon, and Hector the manslayer, pierced by Achilles' lance, and where Simois rolls down submerged beneath his stream those countless shields and helms and all those valiant dead!'

Aeneas was still pouring forth his words when a

howling blast from the north struck squarely his ship's sail and flung the waves sky-high. Oars broke: the bow sheered away; and she took the sea full on her beam. On came, towering, a piled precipice of water. Some of the crew hung poised on wave-crests; others saw the waves sink before them to disclose, below seething water and sand, the very bottom of the sea. The south wind next caught up three other ships, and flung them spinning onto a large spine of rocks, half-submerged in mid-ocean and far out from Italy, where they are called 'the Altars'. The east wind drove three more away from the open sea onto quicksands in shallow water. To the dismay of their friends, the wind ran them aground and built up over them a mountain of sand. One ship carried the Lycians, under their trusty chief Orontes. As Aeneas watched, a gigantic breaker came crashing from its crest onto the stern. The helmsman was whirled head foremost overboard, and fell face downwards. The ship spun three times round where she lay; then a whirlpool caught her and sucked her under. Some of the crew could be seen, one here one there, swimming in the waste of water. Fragments of wreckage, personal equipment, and precious things saved from Troy floated on the waves. The storm had now prevailed against the two stout ships of Ilioneus and of the valiant Achates, and two others also, one carrying Abas and the other the aged Aletes. Every ship had sprung her timbers; the cracks widened, and the deadly sea streamed in.

But meanwhile Neptune had been made aware by the ocean's roaring commotion, and the currents eddying even in the sea's still depths, that a storm had been unleashed. Gravely provoked, he raised his head from the waves and, looking forth serenely high above the surface, he saw Aeneas' fleet scattered and his Trojans overborne by violent waves and all the sky teeming down. He soon realized the trick played by his spiteful sister Juno. He summoned the Winds of the East and the West before him, and straightway spoke:

'So, Winds, is this the length to which your pride of birth prompts you to go? You actually dare, without my sovereign consent, to throw sky and earth into confusion, and raise these mountainous seas? I will show you . . . ! But no, first I had better set the waves at rest; after that you are going to pay dearly for your offence. Make haste now and withdraw. And give your king a message from me. Dominion over the ocean, sanctioned by the ruthless trident, was allotted not to him but to me. His place is the rock's vast cavern where, Wind of the East, you winds have your home. That is the royal court of Aeolus. There he may vaunt his sovereign pride, so long as he keeps the prison of the winds well barred.'

Speaking thus, and quicker than speech, he made the heaving ocean calm. He routed the gathered clouds and brought back the sun. As he did so, Triton and Cymothoe pressed against the ships, and dislodged them from the cutting rocks; and Neptune aided them, levering with his trident. Great sandbanks reappeared, as, lightly skimming the wave-crests in his chariot, he calmed the sea. It had been like a sudden riot in some

great assembly, when, as they will, the meaner folk
forget themselves and grow violent, so that firebrands
and stones are soon flying, for savage passion quickly
finds weapons. But then they may chance to see some
man whose character and record command their re-
spect. If so, they will wait in silence, listening keenly.
He will speak to them, calming their passions and
guiding their energies. So, now, all the uproar of the
ocean subsided. Its Lord, Father Neptune, had only to
look forth over the sea; then under a cloudless heaven
he wheeled his horses, gave them the rein, and let his
willing chariot fly.

Thoroughly exhausted, Aeneas and his men made
efforts to run for the nearest land within reach. They
set course for the coast of Africa. There is a haven
there, at the end of a long sound, quite landlocked by
an island in the shape of two breakwaters, which parts
the waves entering from the open sea and draws them
off into long channels. On each shore a frightening
headland of rock towers massively into the sky; and
the wide expanse of water which they overshadow
is noiseless and secure. Beyond the water a curtain of
trees with quivering leaves reaches downwards, and
behind them is an overhanging forest-clad mountain-
side, mysterious and dark. There is a cave directly in
front at the foot of the cliffs. Inside it are stalactites
and fresh water, and there are seats there, cut in the
living rock, for nymphs have their home in the cave.
Here a tired ship will never need a cable or an anchor
with a fluke to bite and make her fast.

Aeneas, who had reunited only a bare seven ships

out of all his fleet, moved up into the sound. The Trojans, yearning to be on dry land again, disembarked and, delighted to feel the sand under them, lay down, all caked with brine, on the beach. Achates struck a spark from a flint, the first thing to be done; he had leaves there to catch the fire, which he fed by putting dry material around it, and he quickly had a flame in the tinder. Others, although utterly weary from their plight, fetched out some grain which they had saved, though it was the worse for sea-water, and utensils for cooking. They prepared to grind the corn on stone and bake bread.

While they did so, Aeneas climbed a rock commanding a wide unbroken view far across the sea, in the hope of sighting some Trojan ships, wind-battered but afloat, the ship perhaps of Antheus, or of Capys or Caicus with her high, blazoned stern. But there was not a ship to be seen. He could see, however, three stags straying on the shore, and behind them in a long line their whole herd, grazing in a valley. Abruptly he stopped; and quickly he gripped a bow and some arrows, swift to fly, which his faithful Achates had been carrying. His first shots brought the leaders to the ground, stags with tall antlers like tree-branches. Next he turned on the herd, and his arrows stampeded them in confusion among the green forest trees. Aeneas only ceased shooting when he had triumphantly laid on the earth seven weighty carcasses, in number equal to the surviving ships. He now made his way back to the haven, and shared the meat among his company; and with it he apportioned the cargo of wine-casks which with a hero's generosity the kindly Acestes had given them on the beach in Sicily as they embarked. He then spoke to them, to console them in their grief:

'Friends of mine, we have long been no strangers to affliction, and you have had worse than this to bear. Now, as before, Providence will bring your suffering to an end. You have sailed right in among the rocks where Scylla's rabid sea-dogs bark. You have faced the Cyclopes, monsters of the stones. You must revive your spirits and dismiss unhappiness and fear; perhaps one day you will enjoy looking back even on what you now endure. We have forced our way through adventures of every kind, risking all again and again; but the way is the way to Latium, where Destiny offers us rest and a home, and where imperial Troy may have the right to live again. Hold hard, therefore. Preserve yourselves for better days.'

Such were the words he spoke, but he was sick at heart, for the cares which he bore were heavy indeed. Yet he concealed his sorrow deep within him, and his face looked confident and cheerful. The Trojans now prepared to deal with the game on which they were soon to feast. Some of them flayed the hides from the ribs, disclosing the meat. Others then cut the meat into steaks, and spitted it, quivering. Others again found places on the beach for cauldrons, and provided the fires to boil them. Then they ate and restored their strength; stretched on the grass, they filled themselves with old wine and rich venison and feasted till their hunger was gone. When the meal was cleared away, they talked long, in sadness for their lost comrades, poised between the hope that they might possibly be living yet, and the fear that they had reached their life's ending and were beyond all human appeal. More than any other, Aeneas the True sighed within himself for the lot of the fiery Orontes and of Amycus, thinking of each one, or again of some terrible fate which Lycus might have met, and then of Gyas and of Cloanthus, his valiant friends.

They had now finished their meal when Jupiter looked down from heaven's height on the sea where the white wings sail, on the lands flat below, on the coasts, and on the nations of the wide world. He stood in the zenith of the sky and his eyes rested on royal Carthage. Then suddenly, as he pondered gravely on the issues involved, Venus addressed him. She was downcast, and tears stood in her glistening eyes as she spoke: 'Disposer, by eternal decrees, of all life human and divine, you whose bolt of thunder is our dread, how can Aeneas, my dear son, and the other Trojans have given you offence so grave? Often has death visited them; and now, because they make for Italy, all the earth is closed to them. Yet your promise was of Romans, leaders of men, who should one day with the rolling of the years be their descendants, with Teucer's blood, strong once more, running in their veins; they were to discipline all the sea and all lands under their law. Father, what thought has been changing your will? As for me, your promise consoled me for the dread havoc of Troy's fall, since I could weigh against her fate the compensation of this new destiny. But now the Trojans, driven on from disaster to disaster, are still being pursued by the same ill fortune. Monarch Supreme, what end to their ordeals will you grant them? After all, Antenor escaped right through the press of Greeks, and contrived to sail safely up to the head of the Adriatic where the Liburnians hold rule, even reaching the fount of the Timavus, the river through whose nine mouths sea water bursts forth from echoing caverns below, so that ocean's roar is heard on the meadows of the land. And here Antenor actually found a place where Trojans might settle and named his city Padua. He has given its people a Trojan name and hung Trojan weapons on the walls; and there in relief from turmoil he is serenely at peace. Yet we, your own children, having your own permission to climb the very citadel of Heaven, are, all through the anger of One, most monstrously betrayed; our ships are lost, and we are parted far from Italy's coasts. Do you so reward our reverence for you? Is this how you install us in the royalty which is our due?'

The creator of the gods and of human kind smiled on her, with the smile which he wears when he calms the storms and clears the sky. Lightly he kissed his daughter, and then spoke: 'Spare your fears, Cytherean. You have your people's destiny still, and it shall not be disturbed. You shall see your city, see Lavinium's walls, for I have promised them. And you shall exalt to the stars of Heaven your son Aeneas, the great of heart. There is no thought changing my will. But now, because anxiety for him so pricks you, therefore shall I speak of the more distant future, and, turning the scroll of the Fates, awake their secrets. Know, then, that

Aeneas shall fight a great war in Italy and overthrow proud peoples. He shall establish for his warriors a way of life and walls for their defence; and he shall live until the third summer looks on his reign in Latium, and he has passed his third winter in camp since his conquest of the Rutulians. But Ascanius, his young son, who is now given a second name Iulus, having been Ilus as long as the sovereignty of Ilium survived, shall complete in royal power each circling month for thirty long years. Active and vigorous, he shall build Alba Longa to be strong, and thither shall he transfer his rule from its old seat, Lavinium. Here, under a dynasty of Hector's kin, the royal power shall live. Here kings shall reign for a period of three hundred years until one day Ilia, a priestess of the royal blood, shall bear twin sons to Mars. Then shall one Romulus, nursed by a wolf and gay in a red-brown wolfskin, inherit the line. He shall build battlements of Mars; and call his people Romans, after his name. To Romans I set no boundary in space or time. I have granted them dominion, and it has no end. Yes, even the furious Juno, who now wearies sea, earth, and heaven with the strain of fear, shall amend her plans, and she and I will foster the nation which wears the toga, the Roman nation, masters of the world. My decree is made. Time in its five-year spans shall slip by till an age shall come when the House of Assaracus shall crush to subjection even Phthia and illustrious Mycenae, and conquer Argos, and hold mastery there. And then shall be born, of proud descent from Troy, one Caesar, to bound his lordship by Ocean's outer stream and his fame by the

starry sky, a Julius, bearing a name inherited from
Iulus his great ancestor. One day you shall welcome to
Heaven with peace in your heart this Julius, coming
weighted with the spoils of the Orient; and he also
shall be invoked to listen to prayers. Then shall our
furious centuries lay down their warring arms, and shall
grow kind. Silver-haired Fidelity, Vesta, and Quirine
Romulus, with his brother Remus at his side, shall
make the laws. And the terrible iron-constricted Gates
of War shall shut; and safe within them shall stay the
godless and ghastly Lust of Blood, propped on his
pitiless piled armoury, and still roaring from gory
mouth, but held fast by a hundred chains of bronze
knotted behind his back.'

So he prophesied; and he sent Maia's son Mercury
down from Heaven. For the land of Africa, and Carth-
age itself with its newly built defences, were to stand
open to receive the Trojans as guests, and Dido must
not forbid them her territory through ignorance of the
ordained plan. So, oared by his wings, Mercury flew,
striking out across the broad sky, and swiftly he was
there, standing on the coast of Africa. He obeyed his
instructions, and at his divine will the Carthaginians
put from them all thoughts of hostility. Especially he
inspired their queen with a tolerance for the Trojans
and a kindly intent.

Meanwhile Aeneas the True, after a night spent in
thought, decided to walk out in the freshness of the
dawn to investigate this new country, and to see on
what coast the wind had driven him and what creatures
lived there, whether men or wild animals, for he had

noticed that the land was uncultivated; he could then report precisely to his comrades. He left the ships concealed under the trees' mysterious shade, enclosed by the wooded headlands and overhung by the cliff. He stepped out, accompanied by Achates alone and carrying two hunting-spears with broad iron heads quivering in his hand. Under the trees his mother met him. She had a maiden's countenance and a maiden's guise, and carried a maiden's weapons, like some Spartan girl, or like Harpalyce the Thracian who outruns horses till they tire and outstrips even the winged river Hebrus. Slung ready on her shoulder she carried a bow as a huntress would, and she had let her hair stream in the wind; her tunic's flowing folds were caught up and tied, and her knees were bare. She spoke first: 'Ho there, young Sirs! Do you happen to have seen one of my sisters, wearing a quiver and a cloak of spotted lynx-skin, wandering about here, or shouting hard on the track of some foam-flecked boar? If so, tell me where.'

So said Venus. And her son started to answer her: 'No, I have neither seen nor heard any sister of yours ... young lady ... only, how am I to speak of you? You have not the countenance of human kind and your voice has no tones of mortality ... Goddess! For a goddess surely you must be. Not Apollo's own sister? Or one who is kin to the nymphs? Oh, I entreat your favour, whoever you may be, and some relief in our tribulation. Pray tell us under what skies we stand, and where on the world's shores we have been cast. A violent hurricane with its giant waves has driven us hither, and here we now stray, not knowing where we are or who are the inhabitants. If you tell us, we shall offer many victims to you, to fall dead before your altars.'

And Venus answered: 'I am not one to claim any such honour as that. It is the usual habit of Carthaginian maids to carry a quiver, and to wear these high-laced hunting-boots of dark red. The country which you see is ruled by Phoenicians from Tyre, and Agenor's dynasty reigns in their city. But around them is Africa; and no war can subjugate Africans. Queen Dido, who directs the counsels of our state, came here from Tyre, wishing to escape her brother. It is a long and intricate tale of wrong; but I shall trace for you the main events of the story.

'Dido was married to Sychaeus, who was the greatest landowner of all the Phoenicians; and to her sorrow she loved him ardently. She had been a maid when her father gave her to him; her union with him was her first marriage. But she had a brother Pygmalion, who then occupied the throne at Tyre; and he was a monster of unmatched wickedness. A murderous quarrel broke out between the princes. Pygmalion was so blind with lust for gold that he lay in wait for Sychaeus at a holy rite, caught him off his guard, and sacrilegiously struck him down with a dagger-thrust. But he forgot to fear the power of his sister's love. For long Pygmalion concealed his deed, giving Dido false reasons for hope, and with many cruel pretences deluding her heart-sick anxiety. Then, while she slept, the actual spectre of Sychaeus, who was yet unburied, raised before her eyes a face weirdly pale. The wraith revealed the brutal deed at the sacrifice, showed the dagger-wounds in his breast, and disclosed the whole wicked secret of the palace. And he pressed her to leave her homeland and flee in haste. To help her on her journey he told her where there lay in the earth a long-buried and forgotten treasure of gold and silver in great weight. Shocked by the vision, Dido began to prepare for flight, and to gather for her company any who savagely hated or sharply feared the evil king. They assembled, hastily seized some ships which happened to be ready for sailing, and loaded them with the gold. The miserly Pygmalion lost his hoard, for it was conveyed over the ocean; and the whole enterprise was led by a woman. So they reached this place, where you can already see the towering battlements of a new city, Carthage, and its citadel even now being built. They bought as much land "as they could enclose within a bull's hide", and this land is still called "The Hide" after that event. But, tell me, who are you? From what country do you come, and whither do you voyage?'

In answer to her questions, Aeneas spoke with a deep sigh out of his very heart; 'Lady Divine, if I were to start at the beginning and then continue all the chronicle of our ordeals, and if there were the time for you to hear, the star of evening would surely close heaven's gate, and set the day to sleep, before the end. From ancient Troy, if that name has ever chanced to come to your ears, we had been sailing over many strange seas; and then of its own caprice a storm drove us on Africa's coast. I am Aeneas, called the True, and

I carry with me in my ships the gods of our home rescued from the foe. Beyond the sky my fame is known; and I quest for Italy, the land where my family first sprang from supreme Jove. Following my allotted destiny, and shown my way by my divine mother, I sailed forth onto the Phrygian Sea with twenty ships. Scarce seven survive, wrested from the easterly wind and from the waves. And here I wander, in want, unknown, about Africa's wilderness, driven first from Asia and now from Europe too.'

But Venus would not listen to more complaints from him, and she interrupted his lament: 'Whoever you are, They who dwell in Heaven can scarcely hate you, I think. You still breathe and live; and you have reached the city of the Tyrians. Continue on this path till you come to the doorway of the queen's palace. For I can tell you that the winds, veering to the north, have reversed their direction, your ships have been driven to safety, and your comrades have returned to you; if not, then my parents made false claims, and the lessons in prophecy which they gave me have been failures. Look at those twelve swans, gaily in line. Jupiter's eagle had swooped down from the heights of air, and was just now pursuing them across the whole breadth of the sky. And yet you can now see some of the swans alighting in their long ranks on the ground and others looking down from air to earth, where some have already settled. As these swans, now whirring their wings in play, have come safely home, while others flock and freely circle, trumpeting, in the zenith, so too some of your ships with their Trojan crews are safe in harbour, while others with bellying sails are drawing near to the haven's mouth. So just continue your walk, and go ahead where the way leads you.'

So Venus spoke, and as she turned away her loveliness shone, a tint of rose glowed on her neck and a scent of Heaven breathed from the divine hair of her head. Her gown trailed down to her feet; her gait alone proved her a goddess. Aeneas recognized his mother, and as she vanished his cry followed swiftly after: 'Ah, you too are cruel! Why again and again deceive your own son with your mocking disguises? Why may I not join hand to hand, hear you in frankness, and speak to you in return?'

As he reproached her thus he stepped out towards the city walls. For her part Venus fenced the two Trojans with a thick mist, enveloping them by her divine power with a mantle of dense cloud, so that no one might notice or touch them, hinder them, or ask them why they had come. And Venus herself departed soaring high in the air to Paphos. Joyously she returned to her own home where stands her temple and its hundred altars ever warm with the incense of Sheba, and where unceasingly a perfume is breathed from garlands of freshly gathered flowers.

Meanwhile the Trojans hurried along their way, guided by the path. They were now climbing a massive hill which overhung the city and commanded a view of the citadel. Aeneas looked wonderingly at the solid structures springing up where there had once been only African huts, and at the gates, the turmoil, and the paved streets. The Tyrians were hurrying about busily, some tracing a line for the walls and manhandling stones up the slopes as they strained to build their citadel, and others siting some building and marking its outline by ploughing a furrow. And they were making choice of laws, of officers of state, and of councillors to command their respect. At one spot they were excavating the harbour, and at another a party was laying out an area for the deep foundations of a theatre; they were also hewing from quarries mighty pillars to stand tall and handsome beside the stage which was still to be built. It was like the work which keeps the bees hard at their tasks about the flowering countryside as the sun shines in the calm of early summer, when they escort their new generation, now full grown, into the open air, or squeeze clear honey into bulging cells, packing them with sweet nectar; or else take over loads brought by their foragers; or sometimes form up to drive a flock of lazy drones from their farmstead. All is a ferment of activity; and the scent of honey rises with the perfume of thyme.

Aeneas looked up at the buildings. 'Ah, fortunate people,' he exclaimed, 'for your city-walls are already rising!' He walked on, miraculously protected by the cloud, right through the multitudes, mingling among the Carthaginians but noticed by none.

In the heart of the city there was a group of trees giving a wealth of shade. Here the Phoenicians, while they were still shaken after their stormy voyage, had dug from the earth a symbol whose discovery Juno in her queenly knowledge had predicted. It was the head of a spirited horse, and it indicated that the nation would have distinction in war and a plentiful livelihood through centuries to come. At this spot Dido the Phoenician was beginning to build a vast and sumptuous temple for Juno; inside it the dedicated offerings were magnificent, and the goddess's powerful presence could be felt. Bronzen were the raised thresholds to which the stairways led; bronze clamped the beams; and of bronze were the doors which made the hinges groan. Here among the trees a strange experience met Aeneas; for the first time his fears were allayed, and for the first time he dared to hope for life and to feel some confidence in spite of his distress. For as, while waiting for the queen, he inspected everything which there was to see under the mighty temple-roof, in wonder at the city's prosperity, the competitive skill of the craftsmen, and the great scale of their tasks, he saw pictured there the Trojan War, with all the battles round Ilium in their correct order, for their fame had already spread over the world. Agamemnon and Menelaus were there, and Priam; there, too, was Achilles, merciless alike to all three. Aeneas stood still, the tears came, and he said: 'O Achates, where in the world is there a country, or any place in it, unreached by our suffering? Look; there is Priam. Even here high merit has its due; there is pity for a world's distress, and a sympathy for short-lived humanity. Dispel all fear. The knowledge of you shown here will help to save you.' So he spoke. It was only a picture, but sighing deeply he let his thoughts feed on it, and his face was wet with a stream of tears. For he seemed to see again the antagonists warring around the defences of Troy, on one side the Greeks in flight before the charge of Troy's manhood, and on another the Trojans in retreat, and the crested and chariot-borne Achilles in pursuit. Still in tears he recognized in another scene the snow-white tents of Rhesus' encampment, betrayed to Diomede during the early hours of sleep and wrecked by him; and Diomede himself, bloody from the great massacre, was shown driving the fiery horses away to the Greek camp before they could taste the grass of Troyland and drink the water of Xanthus. Elsewhere poor young Troilus was pictured in ill-matched combat with Achilles and in flight before him; he had lost his weapons and his horses had bolted; he was on his back trailing from his empty chariot, but still grasping his reins, with his neck and hair dragging over the ground, and his lance pointing back and tracing lines in the dust. Meanwhile ladies of Troy, with hair thrown free, were seen walking in a mournful procession of supplication; they had been beating their breasts with open hands and they were bearing an offering of a robe to the temple of Pallas; but she was not impartial, for she stood with averted face and looked fixedly at the ground. And Achilles was shown again, this time selling back for gold Hector's lifeless body which he had dragged behind his chariot three times round the walls of Ilium. At that last sight of his friend, a lifeless body despoiled of arms, and of the chariot, and Priam holding forth weaponless hands in entreaty, Aeneas sighed a deep and terrible sigh. He also recognized himself hotly engaged among the Greek chieftains. He saw too the fighting ranks from the Orient, led by black Memnon with his divine

arms. And battle-mad Penthesilea was there, leading
the charge of Amazons carrying their crescent-shields;
in the midst of thousands she blazed, showing her
breast uncovered with a gold girdle clasped below, a
warrior maid daring the shock of combat against men.

As Aeneas the Dardan looked in wonder at these
pictures of Troy, rapt and intent in concentration, for
he had eyes only for them, the queen herself, Dido, in
all her beauty, walked to the temple in state, closely
attended by a numerous, youthful retinue. She was
like Diana when she keeps her dancers dancing on the
banks of Eurotas or along the slopes of Cynthus, with
a thousand mountain-nymphs following in bands on
this side and on that; she is taller than all other god-
desses, as with her quiver slung from her shoulder she
steps on her way, and a joy beyond words steals into
Latona's heart. Like her was Dido, and like her she
walked happily with the throng around her, intent on
hastening the work for her future realm. And then,
facing the Goddess's doorway, under her temple-dome,
with her armed guards about her, she took her seat in
the centre on a raised throne. She was already announc-
ing new laws and statutes to her people and deciding by
her own balanced judgement, or by lot, a fair division of
the toil demanded of them, when suddenly Aeneas
saw, moving towards them and followed by a large
crowd, Antheus, Sergestus, and the bold Cloanthus,
with other Trojans whom the dark hurricane had scat-
tered over the ocean and carried far away to distant
coasts. Amazed at this sight, Aeneas and Achates
both stopped, overjoyed, and yet anxious. They were

in burning haste to clasp their comrades' hands, but disturbed by the mystery of it all. So they made no sign, but, still shrouded by the soft mist, they watched, hoping to discover how their friends had fared, where they had left their ships moored, and why they had come to Carthage; for representatives from every ship were in the crowd, walking amid the noise to the temple, to plead for a sympathetic hearing.

The Trojans now entered, and were allowed to speak directly with the queen. In calm self-possession Ilioneus, the eldest among them, began: 'Your Majesty, to whom Jupiter has granted the right to build your new city, and assigned the duty of curbing lawless tribes with your justice, we are hapless Trojans, whom the winds have carried over every sea. We now entreat you, fend from our ships the terrible flames, and show mercy to a god-fearing breed of men. And indeed consider our predicament more closely. We can hardly have come to devastate your African home with the sword or to lift your cattle and drive them to the beach; as vanquished men we could never be so arrogant and aggressive. No; but there is a region for which the Greeks use the name Hesperia, the Western Land, an ancient land with might in her arms and in her fertile soil. The inhabitants used to be Oenotrians, but it is said that their descendants have now called the country Italy after one of their leaders. To Italy we were setting our course, when suddenly at the rising of Orion, star of storms, the seas ran high. We were carried onto invisible shoals; the gales were headstrong and drove us through seas where the surge boiled over near forbidding rocks. And we few have drifted hither to your coasts. Now tell us – who dwell here? What motherland is so barbarous that it allows such practices? For we are debarred even from such a welcome as barren sands can offer. Your people have started to assault us, and allow us no foothold on the shore. If you have no respect for mortal men or mortal arms, you should at least remember that there are gods who know right from wrong. Aeneas was our king. No one was ever more just than he, nor any greater in righteousness or in prowess at war. If Destiny preserves him still, and if he does not yet lie among the unpitying Shades, but still draws strength from heaven's air, then there is no fear: nor would you ever regret it if you took the first step to compete with him in the exchange of kind-nesses. We also have cities in Sicily, well able to fight; and Acestes is there, a prince of fame from the blood of Troy. And we now desire your permission to beach our storm-damaged ships, and in your forests to shape timbers and strip wood for oars, so that we may sail for Italy and Latium, contented if we may make Italy our destination, and if our king and our comrades are restored to us. If however salvation is denied us, and if you, great and good Chieftain of Trojans, lie deep in the African ocean, and if we can no longer see in Iulus our nation's future, we can yet make for Sicily's narrow sea whence our voyage here began and where a place awaits us, and there take Acestes for our king.' So spoke Ilioneus, and all the other Trojans quickly acclaimed him.

Dido then gave her answer, shortly, with lowered

eyes: 'Trojans, cast fear from your thoughts and entertain no anxieties. Life is hard for us, and this is a new kingdom. That is why I am compelled to take such grave precautions; I have to use guards and keep extensive watch on my frontiers. But who can there be who has never heard of Aeneas and his kindred, of Troy's city, and the valour of her men, or of that war's dreadful blaze? We Phoenicians are not so dull of mind, nor is the Sun when he harnesses his horses so remote from our Tyrian city. Whether your choice is for illustrious Hesperia, the land which Saturn ruled, or for the region by Eryx where Acestes would be your king, I shall help you to depart in safety under my protection and give you aid from my possessions. Or would you rather settle here in my realm on an equal footing with me? Count as your own this city which I am erecting. Beach your ships. There will be no question of making a distinction between Trojans and Tyrians. But now I only wish your king, Aeneas himself, might appear, forced hither like you by the same gales. I shall certainly send reliable men along the coast with orders to range far and wide through Africa, in the hope that he has been cast ashore and is lost in some city or some forest.'

Her speech startled Achates the brave, and Aeneas, his chieftain, too. They had long felt eager to break free from the cloud. It was Achates who spoke first, addressing Aeneas: 'Son of the Goddess, what do you now advise? You see that all is safe, and we have even recovered our comrades and our ships. Only one friend is missing, and we ourselves saw him drowned amidst

the waves. All else agrees with your mother's prophecy.'
Scarcely had he said this when the cloud enveloping
them suddenly parted, and melted away into clear air.
Aeneas checked his walk, and in the bright light he
shone; his face and his shoulders bore a divine beauty,
for his mother had imparted a grace to his hair, she
had shed on him a rich glow of youth, and set a gay
sparkle in his eyes; like the shine which art can give to
ivory, or like silver or marble inlaid in yellow gold.
Then suddenly, to the surprise of all, he addressed the
queen: 'Here am I, in your presence, the one for whom
you all look. I am Aeneas the Trojan, rescued from the
African sea. Queen, you alone have felt pity for the
unutterable ordeals of Troy; and now you would receive
us as partners in your city and your home, us, a mere
remnant left over by the Greeks, and in desperate need,
our strength all drained away by every misfortune of
land and sea. To thank you fitly, Dido, is not within
our power, or the power of any other survivors of the
Dardan race who may still exist dispersed in any part
of the vast world. But if Powers of the Beyond take
thought for the good, if there exists anywhere any
justice at all, or some Intelligence able to know the
right, then may your true reward come from them.
What joyous world gave you your life? Who were great
enough to be parents to one such as you? So long as
rivers shall hurry to the sea, so long as shadows shall
drift over a mountain's shoulder, and so long as the sky
gives pasture to the stars, so long shall live the honour
which is your due, your praises, and your name, to
whatever land I may be called.' So saying, he reached

out with his right hand to his friend Ilioneus and with his left to Serestus, and then to the others, the brave Gyas and the valiant Cloanthus.

At her first sight of Aeneas, Phoenician Dido was awestruck, thinking of the terrible fate which had been his. Then she spoke: 'Son of the Goddess, what is this fortune which has been pursuing you through such fearful perils? What compulsion now flings you on this barbarous shore? Can you truly be that Aeneas whom Venus, the kind life-giver, bore to Dardan Anchises by the waters of Phrygian Simois? Now I myself remember Teucer coming to Sidon, for he had been banished from his own homeland, and wished to win a new realm with aid from Belus my father, who at that time was pillaging Cyprus, the rich island which he had conquered and then held under his sway. Ever since that time I have known of the calamity which befell Troy, and known you, and the Greek princes, by name. Even your enemy, Teucer, gave the Trojans his very highest praise, claiming to be himself descended from the same ancient "Teucrian" stock. Therefore, come, gallant friends, and proceed to my home. A fortune not unlike yours has harassed me, and led me, too, through many tribulations, to rest at long last in this country. My own acquaintance with misfortune has been teaching me to help others who are in distress.' After speaking so to Aeneas she led him into the palace. As she walked she gave orders for temple-offerings in thanks to the Gods. She also remembered to send twenty bulls to Aeneas' friends on the shore with a hundred bristling hogs' backs, a hundred fat lambs with their ewes, and the god's joyous gift of wine. Inside the palace the preparations were regally sumptuous. They were making ready a banquet in the central hall. There was drapery artistically worked in princely purple, a massive array of silver on the tables, and gold plate engraved with the heroic deeds of this people's ancestors, in a long succession of historic events throughout all the generations since their nation's birth.

But Aeneas found that his love for his son would not let his mind rest. He sent Achates swiftly to the ships, with instructions to tell Ascanius the news and to bring him to the walled city, for the loving father's every thought was fixed on Ascanius. Achates was also to fetch presents, things rescued from the fall of Troy; a figured gown stiff with gold lace, and a mantle hemmed with a yellow thistle-pattern, both garments which had graced Argive Helen, fine gifts from her mother Leda which she had carried off from Mycenae when she first started for Troy and her wicked marriage. Aeneas added a sceptre, once borne by Priam's eldest daughter Ilione, a necklace shaped like a row of mulberries, and a double diadem of gold set with jewels.

Achates hastened to obey and was soon on his way to the ship. But meanwhile Venus was pondering new plans and new devices. She decided to make Cupid assume the form and features of the charming Ascanius, and go in place of him; he should give Dido the presents, and as he did so enflame her with a distraction of love, and entwine the fire of it about her very bones. For Venus could not help fearing the uncertainty of a home menaced by Phoenician duplicity; Juno's savage will tormented her, and as night drew on her anxiety returned. Therefore she spoke to her winged son: 'Son, you alone are my strength and all my might is in you. Son, you even scorn the Father's Typhoean thunderbolts. Now I appeal to you, and humbly pray to your divine majesty for aid. You know how your brother Aeneas has travelled storm-tossed on the ocean round every coast solely on account of merciless Juno's persistent hate; you have often sympathized with me in my sorrow. And now Phoenician Dido detains him and talks to him, coaxing him to stay with her. I am anxious about the outcome of any entertainment which Juno sanctions; she will certainly not be slow to act at this critical moment. Therefore I plan to forestall her by a trick of my own and enclose the queen in such a girdle of flames that no act of divine power may divert her from submitting, as I intend, to a fierce love for Aeneas. To enable you to effect this, listen now to my plan. Aeneas his dear father has now sent for the young prince who is my own greatest love; and he is now preparing to go to the Phoenician city with gifts, things saved from the fire of Troy and from the ocean perils. I shall lull him into a profound sleep, and then hide him away in my hallowed precinct high up on Cythera or at Idalium; for otherwise he might learn of the trick or appear suddenly while it is being played. You must just for one night assume his shape as a disguise, and wear his familiar features; after all, he is a boy like you. Then, during the royal entertainment, when the wine is flowing, and Dido in her great happiness clasps you to her, embracing you and planting on you her sweet kisses, you shall breathe into her invisible fire, and poison her, without her knowing.' Cupid obeyed his dear mother's command. He took off the wings from his shoulders, and in great amusement copied Iulus' way of walking. Venus now poured delicious and pervasive sleep into Iulus, and holding him closely and caressingly she carried him by her divine power to Idalium's wooded upland, where soft amaracus guarded him amid flowers and shade, and spread sweetness with the perfume which it breathed.

The obedient Cupid was soon on his way carrying the royal gifts for the Queen of Carthage, and happy in the guidance of Achates. When he arrived, the queen had just composed herself, proudly curtained on her golden seat in the centre. And here Troy's chieftain Aeneas and all the manhood of Troy forgathered, and took their places on coverlets of purple. Attendants held water for them to wash their hands, passed them bread in baskets, and brought napkins of soft material. Beyond, within the palace, waited fifty serving maids, each at her station, whose office it was to replenish the capacious store-rooms and rekindle the hearth-fire of the home. There were a hundred other maids and a hundred manservants, all matched for age, to load the food onto the tables and set forth the drink. Many Carthaginians, who had been invited to take their places on the embroidered banquet-seats, entered through the festal doorways. They wondered at the gifts from Aeneas, and at Iulus – the divinity in disguise – now wearing a flush of emotion and speaking in his assumed character. They admired the sceptre and the mantle hemmed with the yellow thistle-pattern. But beyond all the rest the unhappy Phoenician Dido, condemned now to sure destruction, could not satisfy her longing. She gazed, and the fire in her grew; she was affected equally by the boy and by the beautiful gifts. Cupid had been clinging to Aeneas and embracing him with his arms around his neck, expressing great love for his supposed father. Then he crossed to the queen. Dido's eyes and her whole mind were fixed on him, and at times she would fondle him and hold him close to her, for she could not know, poor Dido, how mighty a god was entering her. And then he, remembering the wish of his mother the Cyprian, began gradually to dispel from Dido all thought of Sychaeus; and he assailed that heart of hers so long inactive, and her brain, so unused to these thoughts, with the thrill of a living love.

The banquet came to its first pause, and tables were removed. They set in place great bowls of wine, and filled them to the brim. Loud talk broke out in the palace, and the voices rolled through the hall's great spaces. There were lamps hanging from the gold-panelled ceiling, and a blaze of candles vanquished the darkness. The queen asked for a jewelled drinking-bowl of heavy gold. She filled it with wine of full strength, as the first Belus and all his successors had filled it often before. There was a call for silence in the palace, and she spoke:

'Jupiter, you who are said to have created the laws

of hospitality, may it be your wish to make this day a
fortunate day for the Phoenicians and for the exiles
from Troy, a day to be remembered by our descendants.
May Bacchus, giver of joy, and Juno the generous,
grant their blessing. Phoenicians, show your good will,
and make our gathering festive.' So saying, she poured
out a drink-offering onto the table. After the libation
she first touched the drink with her own lips, and
passed it then to Bitias, with a challenge. He boldly
drank all the foaming bowl, soaking himself from the
full gold vessel. Other Phoenician lords drank after
him. And Iopas of the long hair took his lyre bound
with gold, and his music rang. The great master, Atlas,
had been his teacher; he sang now of the wandering
moon and the labouring sun; of the origin of men and
of beasts, of rain, of fire, of Arcturus and the Hyads
which foretell the rain, and of the two Bears. His song
told why on each winter day the sun so hastens to dip
in ocean, and told of the cause which then retards the
nights and makes them slow. The Phoenicians cheered
and cheered again, and the Trojans applauded with
them. And the doomed Dido herself spent the whole
night in talk of many kinds, drinking deep of her love.
She asked question after question about Priam and
Hector; she asked what arms the Son of the Dawn had
carried when he came to Troy, and enquired now of
the quality of Diomede's horses, and now of the stature
of Achilles. Then she said: 'But, come! You must tell
me, guest of mine, the whole story from the beginning,
of the trap which the Greeks set, the calamity which

befell your people, and your own wanderings; for it is now the seventh summer of your roaming over the land and sea throughout the world.'

BOOK TWO
The Fall of Troy

They fell silent, every one, and each face was turned intently towards him. From high on the dais Aeneas, Troy's Chieftain, began to speak:

'Majesty, too terrible for speech is the pain which you ask me to revive, if I am to tell how the Greeks erased the greatness which was Troy and the Trojan Empire ever to be mourned. I witnessed that tragedy myself, and I took a great part in those events. No one could tell the tale and refrain from tears, not even if he were a Myrmidon or a Dolopian, or some soldier of the unpitying Ulysses. Besides, the moist air of late night falls swiftly from the sky. The stars are setting and they remind us that we too must rest. Still, if you are truly anxious to learn what befell us and to hear a short account of Troy's last agony, even though I shudder at the memory and can hardly face its bitterness, I shall begin.

'The Greek commanders, disappointed by fate and broken by the war as year after year slipped by, built a giant of a wooden horse, making its flanks from a trellis of sawn firwood. The craftsmanship was divinely inspired by Minerva. They pretended that it was an offering to secure their homeward voyage; and such

Virgil

was the rumour which spread. Then they drew lots, and unobserved, locked a party of picked men in its dark interior till the horse's cavernous womb was full of armed soldiers.

'Within sight of Troy is the island of Tenedos. In the days of Priam's Empire it had wealth and power and was well known and famous, but there is nothing there now, except the curve of the bay affording its treacherous anchorage. The Greeks put to sea as far as Tenedos, and hid from sight on its lonely beaches. We thought they had sailed for Mycenae before the wind and gone home. So all the land of Troy relaxed after its years of unhappiness. We flung the gates open and we enjoyed going to look at the unoccupied, deserted space along the shore where the Greek camp had been. Yes, here the Dolopians had their station. And there camped the merciless Achilles. Over there the ships were moored; and this was the usual ground for pitched battle. Some of us looked in awed wonder at that massive horse, the gift for Minerva the never-wed, which was to be our destruction. Thymoetes, perhaps out of treason or perhaps because Troy's fate was already fixed, was the first to make a proposal: we should tow the horse inside the city-walls and leave it standing on our citadel. But others, among them Capys, judged more wisely, for they suspected treachery in anything freely offered by Greeks. They advised us to destroy it by casting it down into the sea or by setting fire to it and burning it; or else to pierce it and tear open the hidden lair within. The rest were divided in keen support of one proposal or the other.

36

'But there, in front of all, came Laocoon, hastening furiously down from the citadel with a large company in attendance. While still far off he cried: "O my unhappy friends, you must be mad indeed. Do you really believe that your enemies have sailed away? Do you think that a Greek could offer a gift without treachery in it? Do you know Ulysses no better than that? Either some of their men have been shut inside this timber-work and are now hiding in it, or the horse itself is a machine for overcoming our walls, perhaps to pry somehow into our homes or threaten Troy from its height; or it hides some other confusion for us. Trojans, never trust that horse. Whatever it proves to be, I still fear Greeks, even when they offer gifts." As he spoke, he powerfully heaved a great spear at the horse's side, into the firm timber-work of its rounded belly, and there it stood, quivering. At the impact, the echoing spaces of the cavernous womb growled and rang; and if the destined will of Heaven had not been set against us, and our own reason had not been deranged, Laocoon had surely driven home a thrust till the iron tore open the Greek lair. Troy would then have survived till now; and, O proud Citadel of Priam, you would have been standing yet.

'But another figure suddenly appeared, a young stranger, with his arms shackled behind him. Some Trojan shepherds had chanced on him, and now with much shouting they were hurrying him to King Priam. He had in fact waited for them to capture him. His set purpose was to lay Troy open to the Greeks; relying on his own cool nerve, he was ready for either outcome, whether success in his deceptions or certain death. Anxious to look at him, the young Trojans came hastening up and gathered round, outdoing each other in mockery of the captive. You are now to hear how the Greeks tricked us. From this one proof of their perfidy you may understand them all.

'The captive halted confused and defenceless in our midst where all could see him. His frightened eyes glanced round the lines of Trojans. Then he spoke: "Oh, is there anywhere now left on land or sea where I can find refuge? No, there is no hope at all for me in this extreme of misery. Nowhere among the Greeks have I any place; and meanwhile the Trojans are no less hostile and vengefully demand my blood!" This piteous talk changed our mood and checked each violent impulse. We pressed him to tell us his nationality and his errand and to explain why he had dared to face the risks of capture. At last he laid his dread aside, and answered: "Whatever is to happen I shall tell your Majesty the whole story, and it will be true. First, I admit that I am of Greek nationality; my name is Sinon. Fortune may have made of me a man of sorrows, but even her malice can never change me into a man of faithlessness and lies. Now there may perhaps have come to your ears some mention of Palamedes, a king of great military renown, whom, in spite of his innocence and merely because he opposed this war, the Greeks arraigned on a monstrous charge of treason and executed; though now, when he has passed from the light, they mourn him. When I was still very young, my father, who was not rich, sent me here to the war to be aide to Palamedes, for we were close relatives. Now as long as Palamedes remained secure in his royal station and exerted influence among the kings in council, I also enjoyed some distinction and respect. But when, through the jealous deceit of Ulysses, which will be no surprise to you, Palamedes passed from the world of the living, I was crushed, and lived a weary life of obscurity and grief, in lonely bitterness at the fate of my innocent friend. But I must have been mad, for I did not keep this resentment to myself. Indeed, I vowed vengeance upon them, should I ever return after victory to my native Argos and have my chance. By my words I roused against myself a fury of hate; and I was already on the slippery path to destruction, for from then on Ulysses never ceased intimidating me with some new accusation, spreading suggestive hints among our army, and coldly planning to strike me down. Nor did he ever rest until, making Calchas his accomplice – but what use is it for me now to trace the course of this story? You do not want to hear it, and I only waste words, for you naturally class all Greeks together, and it is enough for you that I carry the name of Greek. So it is more than time for you to be taking your vengeance on me. How that would please the man from Ithaca! And what would the sons of Atreus not give in return for it!"

'This of course made us most anxious to question Sinon and press him to explain; we had no idea to what lengths of wickedness Greek cunning could go. He, subtle actor that he was, nervously continued his tale:

'"Several times the Greeks, wearied by so long a

war, wanted to abandon it, leave Troyland, and some-
how effect a retreat. And how I wish they had done
so! But each time as they were starting tempestuous
seas checked them and contrary winds filled them with
alarm; and more than ever, when this horse now stood
complete in its texture of maple-planks, did storm and
rain shriek across the sky. In our anxiety, we sent
Eurypylus to question Apollo's oracle, and he returned
from the shrine with this terrible message: 'Greeks,
you shed blood when you sacrificed a maiden to calm
the winds for your original voyage to Troy. You must
shed blood again to win your return, for only the
sacrifice of a Greek life can make your prospect fair.'
When these words reached the army, they were terror-
stricken, and icy shudders ran down their spines. No
one could say on whom the choice of Apollo would
fall, and who was to meet his doom. At this moment
the Ithacan forced Calchas our prophet to come with
him before us all. There was uproar. He openly pressed
him to explain the meaning of the god's demand. Many
were already predicting that I was to be the victim of
this brutal and cunning wickedness, but they awaited
the outcome without protest. For ten days Calchas
maintained a silent reserve, refusing to let any word of
his betray anyone to death by sacrifice. But the loud
insistence of the Ithacan prevailed; conniving at last,
the prophet broke his silence, and marked me for the
altar. The others all approved, for, each having feared
that this fate would be his, they were relieved when it
fell to some other wretch. The day of horror quickly
came. The ritual implements of my sacrifice were made

ready, with the usual salted grain and the headbands round my forehead. Well, as I can now admit, I burst from my confinement and made my escape from death. All that night I hid unseen amid the reeds in the mud by the lake, hoping against hope that they would sail. I could no longer believe that I should ever again see the ancient land of my home or my dear children or the father for whom I yearned. Probably the Greeks will now wreak vengeance on all of them for my escape, punishing my crime by killing my helpless family. I now entreat your Majesty, in the name of the High Gods and of all those Powers from whom no truth is hidden, yes, and in the name of any fidelity which may remain inviolate in the world of men, have pity on one whose ordeal has been so terrible, and who has borne what none should have to bear."

'These tears gained him his life, and we even began to feel sorry for him. Priam set the example, giving orders for him to be relieved of the taut ropes and handcuffs. He spoke kindly to him: "Well, whoever you are, there are no Greeks here; forget them quickly and become one of us. Now answer my questions, truthfully and thoroughly. What was their purpose in erecting this massive structure in the shape of a giant horse? Who suggested it and what is it for? What is supposed to be its use either in ritual or as an engine of war?"

'That was all. Sinon, adept in deception and with all the cunning of a Greek, raised his hands, newly freed from the bonds, palm-upwards towards the heavens and spoke: "Bear me now witness, eternal

Starfire, Majesty never profaned; bear me witness, altar, and ghastly knives, and holy headbands of the sacrificial victim which I myself have worn. It cannot be sin for me to break obligations which are only sacred among Greeks. It cannot be sin for me to show my hatred for them, and expose to daylight what the Greeks are hiding; for I can incur no guilt under any law of my homeland. If I bring you truth and repay you well, all that I ask of Troy, if she is not broken, is, not to break her faith, but honour her plighted word.

'"From the start of the war the only hope of victory which the Greeks ever had lay in help from Pallas. But there came that night when sacrilegious Diomede and Ulysses, always quick to invent new crimes, crept up to wrest Troy's talisman, the image of Minerva, from your hallowed temple, cut down the sentries guarding the upper citadel, seized the holy figure, and actually touched the virgin headband of our goddess with blood still on their hands. From that night the prospects of the Greeks receded like an ebbing tide and trickled away; their strength was gone; the heart of the goddess set hard against them.

'"Of this she herself gave certain proof by marvels. The image had hardly been set down in the Greek camp when flickering flames shone in its staring eyes, a salt sweat ran down over its limbs, and three times it lunged miraculously from its base, shield in hand, lance quivering. Calchas, under inspiration, advised the Greeks to attempt an immediate escape across the sea, since no Greek attack could now demolish Troy's defences, unless they first went back to Argos to receive again the promise of divine favour which freighted their shapely galleys when they first crossed the sea. So now they have sailed back to their home-city Mycenae only to re-arm, and to re-enlist their divine allies, and they will soon traverse the ocean again, to startle you with their reappearance. Such was the plan which Calchas pieced together for them from the omens. On his advice they erected this effigy of a horse, to make amends for their profanation of Pallas' image and to expiate the burden of their guilt. At the same time he made them build it of this massive size, a giant structure of hard oak planks, and raise it high towards the heavens, to prevent it from being admitted through the gates or hauled over the walls. If it were, it would only guard your people in the shelter of your ancient faith. For if hand of yours damaged the offering to Minerva, a terrible destruction, such as I would to Heaven Calchas himself might suffer, would come on Priam's empire and the Trojans; but if the horse climbed into your city with help from your hands, then Asia would be free to launch an invasion up to the very ramparts of Pelops, and such would then be the destiny awaiting our grandsons."

'So we gave Sinon our trust, tricked by his blasphemy and cunning. His ruse, and his artificial tears, entrapped men whom neither Tydeus' son nor Larissaean Achilles could subdue, for all their ten years of war and their fleet of a thousand keels.

'But now to our distress a far more momentous and frightful experience befell us, and the unexpected shock of it disordered our minds. Laocoon, who had been chosen by lot to be priest of Neptune, happened at this moment to be sacrificing a fine bull at the altar of the cult, when, and I sicken to recall it, two giant arching sea-snakes swam over the calm waters from Tenedos, breasting the sea together and plunging towards the land. Their fore-parts and their blood-red crests towered above the waves; the rest drove through the ocean behind, wreathing monstrous coils, and leaving a wake that roared and foamed. And now, with blazing and blood-shot eyes and tongues which flickered and licked their hissing mouths, they were on the beach. We paled at the sight and scattered; they forged on, straight at Laocoon. First each snake took one of his two little sons, twined round him, tightening, and bit, and devoured the tiny limbs. Next they seized Laocoon, who had armed himself and was hastening to the rescue; they bound him in the giant spirals of their scaly length, twice round his middle, twice round his throat; and still their heads and necks towered above him. His hands strove frantically to wrench the knots apart. Filth and black venom drenched his priestly hands. His shrieks were horrible and filled the sky, like a bull's bellow when an axe has struck awry, and he flings it off his neck and gallops wounded from the altar. The pair of serpents now made their retreat, sliding up to the temple of heartless Minerva high on her citadel, where they vanished near her statue's feet behind the circle of her shield. At this an access of utter panic crept into every trembling heart. Men said that Laocoon had deserved to pay for his wickedness in damaging the sacred woodwork with his lance, when he made his sinful cast at the horse's side. All were loud in their desire for the horse to be towed to its rightful place and prayers of entreaty to be offered to Minerva's might.

'We cut through our walls and threw our defences open. All set to work with zest. Rollers for smooth running were placed under the horse's feet and hempen ropes tied round its neck. That engine of doom, pregnant with armed men, mounted our walls. Boys and unwedded girls sang hymns around it, happy in the hope that the very touch of the ropes would bring them luck. The brute climbed on; then sank menacingly to rest right inside Troy. O Ilium where gods had their home, O my land and ramparts which Trojans held in glorious defence! Four times the horse halted in the gateway, and each time weapons clanged within it. But we remained witless, and blind, and mad; we pressed ahead, and stationed the malignant horror within our consecrated citadel. Cassandra, whom her own god had ruled that no Trojan should believe, let her lips utter once again the truth of what destiny had in store. We, poor fools, spent this our last day decorating with festal greenery every temple in our town.

'Meanwhile the sky circled round, and night fell over the ocean, wrapping in a single darkness the earth, the high heaven, and the treachery of the Greeks. There was no sound from the Trojans, stretched out weary in the embrace of sleep about the fortress-city. By then the whole Greek fleet was sailing from Tenedos with all ships in ordered lines under the friendly secrecy of a hidden moon toward the old landing-place. Suddenly the king's ship displayed a fire signal; and Sinon under the divine protection of an unjust destiny stealthily removed the horse's pinewood bars and released the Greeks from their confinement. The horse stood open, restoring them to the fresh air. Glad to be free, forth from the timber cavity came the two chieftains, Thessandrus and Sthenelus, and then the merciless Ulysses, sliding down a rope dropped from the horse. Next came Acamas and Thoas, Neoptolemus of Peleus' line, and Machaon in the lead; Menelaus, too, and Epeus, the very craftsman who had made the device. They marched on a city buried in a sleep deepened by wine. The sentries were cut down, the gates stood open, they admitted all their comrades, and the forces were joined, as planned.

'It was the hour when divinely given rest first comes to poor human creatures, and creeps over them deliciously. In my sleep I dreamed that Hector stood there before my eyes. He looked most sorrowful, and was weeping plenteous tears. He was filthy with dust and blood, as he had been that day when he was dragged behind the chariot, and his feet were swollen where they had been pierced by the thongs. And, oh, how harrowing was the sight of him: how changed he was from the old Hector, back from battle wearing the spoils of Achilles, or that time when he had just flung Trojan firebrands onto the Greek ships! Now his beard was ragged and his hair clotted with blood, and all those wounds which he had sustained fighting to defend the walls of his homeland could still be seen. I dreamed that I spoke first, weeping and forcing myself to find words for this sad meeting: "Light of the Dardan

Land, Troy's surest hope, what held you from us so long? How we have waited for you, Hector! From what bourne do you come? We are weary now, and many of your folk are dead. We and our city have had many adventures, many trials. To think that we may look on you again! But what can have so shamefully disfigured your princely countenance? And why these wounds which I see?" He made no reply and gave no attention to my vain questions, but with a deep, choking sob he said: "Son of the Goddess, make your escape quickly from the fires around you. Your walls are captured, and all Troy from her highest tower is falling; Priam and our dear land have had their day. If any strong arm could have defended our fortress, surely mine would have defended it. But now Troy entrusts to you her sanctities and her Guardians of the Home. Take them with you to face your destiny, and find for them the walled city which one day after ocean-wandering you shall build to be great, like them." As he spoke, with his own hands he fetched out from the inner shrine the holy headbands, Vesta in whom dwells power, and her hearth-fire which burns for ever.

'Confused cries of anguish now began to reach me from inside our city. The house of my father Anchises lay back, secluded behind a screen of trees; but even there the battle-noise grew louder and louder, till the air was thick with its terror. I was startled out of my sleep, and climbing to the highest point of the roof stood listening keenly. It was like fire catching a corn-field when wild winds are blowing, or like the sweep of a mountain torrent in flood, flattening smiling crops for which oxen had toiled, and bringing whole forests down, while some shepherd standing high on a crag of rock hears the roar in helpless wonder. There was no doubt now as to the truth; it was at once clear how the Greeks had outwitted us. Already the fire had vanquished the broad mansion owned by Deiphobus, and down it crashed. Ucalegon's, closest to it, was already ablaze. The wide Straits of Sigeum were lit up by the burning. Shouts arose and trumpets rang. Out of my senses, I grasped my arms; not that I had any plan for battle, but simply a burning desire to muster a band for fighting, and rally with my comrades at some position of defence. Frantic in my fury I had no time for decisions; I only remembered that death in battle is glorious.

'But now appeared Panthus, Othrys' son, who was priest of Apollo's temple on the citadel. He had escaped the Greek missiles and was running wildly to our doorway, leading his little grandson by the hand and carrying his sacred vessels and figures of his defeated gods. "Panthus," I cried, "Which is the point of greatest danger? Where do we take our stand?" I had hardly spoken when with a moan he replied, "The last day has come for our Dardan land. This is the hour which no effort of ours can alter. We Trojans are no more: no more is Ilium; no more the splendour of Teucrian glory. All now belongs to Argos; it is Jupiter's remorseless will. For the Greeks are masters of our city and already it burns. The Horse stands towering within our ramparts, streaming armed men; and Sinon glorying in his triumph stirs the blaze. The main array of the

Greeks, all those thousands who came from imperial Mycenae, mass at the open gates. Others have blocked the narrow streets with weapons levelled, and their unsheathed swordpoints, a flickering line of steel, stand instantly ready to kill. Only the foremost sentinels at the gates attempt resistance, and they fight blind."

'These words from Panthus, together with some impulse from above, sent me dashing into the fires and the fight, guided by the roaring, the shouts which rose to heaven, and the dark instinct of revenge. I was joined by Ripheus and the mighty warrior Epytus who came up looming through the moonlight. With them were Hypanis and Dymas, and young Coroebus; and they all stood together at my side. Coroebus was a son of Mygdon, and he had come to Troy as it chanced a few days before, because he hoped to win the hand of Cassandra, whom he loved with a mad and burning love, by an offer of aid to Priam and our nation; and it was disastrous for him that he had not heeded the wild warnings of his princess. Seeing them all shoulder to shoulder, dauntless for battle, I called out to them: "Men, valiant hearts, though valour cannot help us now, if your ardour is set on following the path of daring to the very end – you see for yourselves how our fortune stands. Those gods on whom our power hitherto depended have forsaken their altars and their shrines and are gone forth from us; the city which you would rescue is already ablaze; and it is for us to plunge amid the spears and die. Nothing can save the conquered but the knowledge that they cannot now be saved."

'That gave to their proud hearts the strength of desperation. Like wolves out for prey in a thick mist, forced blindly onwards by hunger's incessant torment and the thought of their cubs left behind and waiting with parched throats for their return, we drove on amid the spears to certain death, taking the way to the centre of Troy and passing directly through the enemy, shadowed by the soft, black wings of the darkness.

'No tongue could describe the carnage of that night and its orgy of death; no tears could match such agonies. An ancient city was falling and the long years of her empire were at an end. Everywhere the dead lay motionless about the streets, in the houses, and on those temple stairs which our tread had reverenced so long. Nor was it only the Trojans who paid the penalty by their blood. Sometimes prowess revived even in the vanquished, and then it was Greeks who fell despite their victory. All was a torment of suffering and fear, with death in a thousand forms.

'The first to meet our band was Androgeos, who appeared with a strong force of Greeks beside him, and carelessly mistook us for some of his own side on the march. He even gave us a friendly hail: "Make haste, my comrades! Why are you late, and idling along like this? Are you only now arriving from the tall ships, when already the centre of Troy is afire and the rest are looting and pillaging?" But he received no assurance in answer; and he had hardly spoken when he realized that he had stumbled right into the enemy. He shrank back at the shock, and checked his words; he was like a man who, as he puts his weight to the ground, finds that he has trodden on a snake lying unseen amid wild brambles, and recoils in sudden fright as it angrily raises the swelling metal-blue of its neck. Just so did Androgeos tremble at the sight of us and try to retreat. But we charged, and our counter-attack enveloped the Greeks, who did not know the ground and were seized by panic. We bore them down; our first enterprise had met with luck. It was now that the high-spirited Coroebus, triumphant at this success, cried, "Friends, let us accept this first hint from Fortune, and win to safety, guided by her smile. We must exchange shields with the Greeks and wear their badges. Who cares whether what we do to an enemy is treachery or valour? The Greeks shall give us the arms which we need." With these words he began equipping himself with Androgeos' plumed helmet and his nobly blazoned shield; and he girded the Argive sword to his waist. Ripheus, Dymas, and all our company followed his example in high spirits, arming themselves with the newly won spoils of the vanquished. So we strode on, mingling with the Greeks and submitting to alien deities. In the utter darkness we were often plunged into conflict and whenever we fought we despatched many a Greek to the land of the dead. Others scattered and fled to their ships, running to the beaches for safety. Some were even cowardly enough to climb again into the capacious horse and hide as before in its belly.

'Sad to say, even trust in Heaven is forbidden when Heaven itself declines the trust. For there before us Priam's own daughter Cassandra was being dragged from the very shrine of Minerva's temple; her hair was astream, and she could only turn her burning eyes helplessly to heaven, for bonds prevented her from raising her delicate hands in prayer. Coroebus could not bear to see her in this plight. The madness entered him, and he plunged among the Greeks to certain death. Our whole force followed, charging with massed weapons. And now for the first time we were attacked by our own side, and came under a shower of spears from the temple-roof. They had mistaken our Greek crests and the Greek shape of our arms; and so started a tragic massacre. The Greeks roared with indignation at the rescue of the girl. Concentrating from all around, they came on, Ajax the most furious of them all, with Agamemnon, Menelaus, and all the Dolopian army; like winds in conflict when a hurricane bursts, winds of the west and of the south, and the east wind exultant on horses of the dawn, while forests howl, and Nereus, making violent play with his trident amid the foam, stirs the sea to its very floor. We were even confronted again by some of those whom in the darkness we had sent hurrying away in the night-shadows and pursued in flight through all Troy; they were the first to see through our deceptive weapons and shields; and they had noticed that our language was foreign to them. We were quite helpless, and weight of numbers bore us down. Coroebus was the first to fall; he died by the hand of Peneleos beside the altar of the goddess mighty in arms. Ripheus fell also, he, the most just of all Trojans, who never wavered from the right; yet the gods regarded not his righteousness. Hypanis, too, and Dymas died, pierced by their friends; and you, Panthus,

even all your holiness and Apollo's own emblem on
your brow could not save you in your falling. Ashes of
Ilium, O last flame burning all that was dear to me,
bear witness that at your setting I never shrank from
any risk of combat amid the spears, but earned at Greek
hands the death which fate denied me. And now we
were forced apart. With me were Iphitus, ageing and
slow, and Pelias who was hampered by a wound from
Ulysses. Guided by shouts we made direct for Priam's
palace. There the ferocity of the fight was intense
indeed; all the warring and the slaughter elsewhere in
the city were nothing to it. We faced Mars in his full
fury. The Greeks were dashing to the building, and
thronging round the entrance with their shields locked
together over their backs; ladders were already firmly
in place against the walls, and the attackers even now
putting their weight on the rungs close to the door-
lintels. Holding shields on their left arms thrust for-
ward for protection, with their right hands they grasped
the roof. To oppose them the Trojans, on the brink of
death and knowing that their plight was desperate,
sought to defend themselves by tearing up tiles from
the roof-tops of houses and even loosening towers to
use as missiles. And they sent rolling down on the
enemy gold-plated roof-beams, the pride of the ancient
Trojans. Some of them, with sword-points bared,
blocked the entrances and, closing their ranks, guarded
them well. We felt a new surge of courage and deter-
mined to aid the palace, bring relief to the defenders
and lend fresh vigour to the vanquished.

'There was a secret access to the palace gained

through a concealed entrance, a doorway never noticed by passers-by, which communicated between the mansions of King Priam's family. In the days of our empire poor Andromache would often walk this way, unattended, to Hector's people, when she took little Astyanax to see his grandfather. Here I entered, and climbed to the highest point of the sloping roof, from which the unhappy Trojans were busy casting their unavailing missiles. Now there was a tower, built on the roof of another structure high into the air above a precipitous drop, whence we used to look out over all Troyland and see the Greek camp and fleet. We hacked with iron blades all round it where the upper storeys presented loosened joints. We wrenched it free from its high position, and thrust it over. Down it suddenly slid with a roar trailing havoc behind, and crashed on many ranks of the attackers. But others took their places, and their showers of stones and the missiles of every kind never slackened.

'In the front of the entrance-hall, and right in the gateway of the palace, stood Pyrrhus, a figure of armed insolence sparkling in a sheen of bronze; like a snake which after a winter spent hidden below ground, swollen from a fare of poisonous weeds, now emerges into the light, and shedding its slough becomes shiningly fresh and young, then raises its breast tall to the sun, coils a slithering back, and sets flickering a triple tongue. With Pyrrhus were the gigantic Periphas, Automedon the squire and charioteer of Achilles, and all the company from Scyros. Together they moved up to the building and cast firebrands to the roof. Pyrrhus, who was leading, seized an axe and smashed in the stout door, rending the bronze-plated hinge-posts from their sockets; soon he had hacked out a panel and hewn a hole through the door's tough oak, making in it a great gaping window. The interior stood revealed. A long vista of galleries was suddenly exposed, and the private home of King Priam and the kings before him came into view, with armed defenders standing on the entrance-threshold.

'Inside the palace there was sobbing and a confused and pitiful uproar. The building rang from end to end with the anguished cries of women. Shouts rose to the golden stars. Matrons roved in panic about the vast house, clasping the very pillars in their arms and kissing them. Pyrrhus came on, like Achilles himself in his onset. No bolts or bars, no guards could hold off that attack. The door crumbled under the ceaseless battering. The hinge-posts were wrenched off their sockets, and fell outwards. Utmost violence opened a passage. With access forced, and the first guards cut down, the Greek army flooded in and filled all the palace with its men; more fiercely, even, than some foaming river which breaks its banks and leaps over them in a swirling torrent, and defeats every barrier, till the mad piled water charges on the ploughland and sweeps away with it cattle and their stalls over miles of country. My own eyes saw Pyrrhus with the blood-lust in him, and Agamemnon and Menelaus right inside the gate; they saw Hecuba with her hundred princesses, and Priam himself, fouling with his blood the altar-fire which he had hallowed. Those fifty wedding-rooms with all their hope of lineage to be, and those pillars vaunting their trophies and laden with orient gold, crashed down. The Greeks were masters wherever the fire had not yet come.

'You may also want to know how Priam met his end.

'When he saw that Troy was captured and fallen, that his palace gates were wrenched from their place and the enemy inside his very home, old though he was he vainly drew onto shoulders trembling with age his long unused corslet, and girded at his side an ineffectual sword. And he started hurrying into the thick of the foe seeking to meet his death. In the centre of the palace, and bare to the high heavens above, was a large altar, with near by an old bay-tree bending over it and clasping within its shade the sanctities of the home. Close about this altar, in unavailing sanctuary, with their arms round the statues of our gods, sat Hecuba and her daughters, like doves which have swooped to refuge before a lowering storm. Seeing Priam armed as in his prime Hecuba cried: "O my poor husband, why do you arm like this? What dreadful things would you do? Where are you going in this haste? It is not aid like that, nor any armed defence, which is needed now, and so would it be even if my own Hector had still been with us. No, come to us. This altar will protect us all; or else we shall die together." With these words she drew the ancient king to her, and found a place for him at the holy altar.

'But see, one of Priam's sons, Polites, had just escaped from slaughter at the hands of Pyrrhus and now fled, wounded, through the foemen and their spears down the long colonnades and across the empty halls. Pyrrhus was at his heels in hot fury, with his spear threatening another wound, and each moment he was all but clutching him with his hand. At last Polites came within sight of his parents; and there before their faces he fell, and in copious blood his life streamed away. At that, Priam, even with death all round him and no escape, did not refrain, or spare his anger and his words. "You!" he cried, "if in all Heaven there is any righteousness which takes note of utter wrong, may the gods give you fit thanks and reward you with your due for this wickedness, this foul outrage to a father's countenance, in so making me to see my own son's death before my very eyes! Not so did the great Achilles, whom you falsely claim to be your father, treat Priam when he was his foe; he respected faithfully the suppliant's rights, restored Hector's bloodless body for burial, and gave me safe return to my realm." So said the aged king and he cast his spear. Too weak to wound, it was fended away by the bronze shield: it merely clanged against it and stayed hanging from the shield's centre. Pyrrhus answered: "If so, you shall be my messenger to Achilles my father; remember to tell him of my deplorable deeds and how his son disgraced him. Now die!" So speaking he dragged Priam, quaking and sliding in a pool of his own son's blood, right up to the altar. He twined his left hand in Priam's hair. With his right hand he raised his flashing sword, and buried it to the hilt in his side. Priam's destiny ended here, after seeing Troy fired and Troy's walls down; such was the end fated to him who had augustly ruled a great empire of Asian lands and peoples. His tall body was left lying headless on the shore, and by it the head hacked from his shoulders: a corpse without a name.

'Then for the first time a wild horror gripped me. When I saw King Priam breathing out his life with that ghastly wound, I pictured to myself my own dear father, for both were of an age; and I pictured Creusa, left forlorn, and the pillage of my home, and the fate of my little Iulus. I looked back, to see what force I still had by me. But all had forsaken me. Utterly exhausted they had either flung themselves down from the building, leaping to the ground, or sick with despair they had plunged into the fires. So now I survived entirely alone. And it was then that I saw her, Helen the Tyndarid. As I wandered, peering everywhere in the light cast by the bright blaze, there she was, hiding silent in a place apart by Vesta's door and never stirring. She was dreading equally the bitter hate of the Trojans whose citadel had fallen, and the vengeance due to her from the Greeks and from the fury of the husband whom she had deserted. She had proved a curse alike for Troy and for her homeland; and she lurked concealed, a hated thing, at the altar. Out flashed all the fire in me and I was filled with a rage to avenge my home, and wreak punishment, crime for crime. "So!" thought I, "shall she, unharmed, again see Sparta and Mycenae the land of her birth, and enjoy her state as a victorious queen? Shall she look once more on her husband, her home, her parents and her children, and have round her a retinue of Trojan ladies and lords of our land to serve her? This, after Priam has fallen by the sword, Troy blazed in flames, and our Dardan coast again and again sweated with blood? Not so. There may be no great honour in killing a woman; such a victory can bring no fame. But I shall have some credit for having stamped dead a mortal sin, and punished a wrong which cries out for justice; and it will be joy to have glutted my desire for the vengeance of the fire and satisfied the ashes of all that were ever dear to me!"

'Such were my wild words, for madness had mastered my judgement and gained complete control. But even as I spoke, there in front of me, and more clearly visible to my sight than ever before, appeared my gentle mother, shining on me with pure radiance through the dark, revealing all her divinity, and in loveliness and stature even as the Immortals see her. Catching me with her hand she restrained me. And she spoke to me from her lips of rose: "Son, how can any bitterness awake in you such ungovernable fury? Why this blind anger? And how can your love for us have passed so far from your thoughts? Ought you not first to see where you have left Anchises your age-wearied father, and whether your wife Creusa and your son Ascanius still live? Around them everywhere the hordes of Greeks are prowling, and, if my thought for them had not been their defence, they would by now have been caught by the flames or devoured by the pitiless sword. You must not blame the hated beauty of the Spartan Tyndarid, or even Paris. It was the gods who showed no mercy; it is they who are casting Troy down from

her splendour and power. Now look! For I shall wrest
away all the dank and gloomy mist surrounding you
which veils and dulls your mortal vision. You must
not fear a mother's command, nor decline to obey
her bidding. There, where you see masses of masonry
scattered, stones wrenched from stones, and smoke
and dust billowing upwards together, there Neptune
himself is at work shattering the walls and the founda-
tions dislodged by his mighty trident, and tearing the
whole city from its site. Over there stands Juno most
furious in the van before the Scaean Gates, and with
her sword at her side and violence in her heart she is
calling the marching ranks of her friends from the
Greek ships. Look round! On the citadel's height sits
Tritonian Pallas, light glaring from her garment of
cloud and the merciless Gorgon-head on her breast.
Even the Supreme Father gives renewed courage,
strength and victory to the Greeks, and inspires the
gods themselves to fight against the arms of Troy. Son,
make your escape and flee. Put an end to the striving.
I will be near you everywhere, and set you safe at your
father's door." She finished and then vanished into the
dense shadows of the night. And there were revealed,
oh, shapes of dread, the giant powers of gods not
friendly to my Troy.

'And in truth all Ilium was now, visibly before me,
settling into the fires, and Neptune's own Troy, up-
rooted, was overturning; like an ancient rowan-tree
high up among the mountains, which, hacked with
stroke after stroke of iron axes by farmers vying all
round to dislodge it, begins to tremble and continues

threatening while the crest shakes and the high boughs sway, till gradually vanquished it gives a final groan, and at last overcome by the wounds and wrenched from its place it trails havoc down the mountain-side. I climbed down from the roof, and with the goddess guiding me won my way between the flames and the foes. The weapons let me through; the fires drew back from me.

'But when I reached the threshold of the ancient building which was my father's home, he, whom I had been dearly hoping to find and carry, as my first care, high up into the mountains, refused to go on living in exile after Troy had been razed from the earth. "You others", he said, "your blood does not run the slower for the years, and your strength is unimpaired and still has the vitality which nature gave it. It is for you to hurry your escape. As for me, if the Dwellers in Heaven had wished me to live on, they would have saved my home here for me. I have already once seen Troy sacked and once survived our city's capture. That is enough, and more. Ah, say your goodbyes to me as I lie here just as I am. I shall find death in my own way. The enemy will show pity to me: their thoughts will be set on the spoils. As for burial – that will be a small price to pay; suffering as I do under Heaven's hatred, my age has been prolonged to no purpose through the years, ever since He who is Father of Gods and King of Men blasted me with the winds of his thunder-stroke and touched me with its fire." So he spoke, firm in his resolution, and could not be shaken. We on our side, my wife Creusa, Ascanius, and all our household, wept bitterly and told him with entreaties that he, the head of our family, must not dream of dragging all our hopes down with him like this, and so weighting against us still more the doom which bore so heavily upon us. But he still refused, and would not stir from his seat or change his purpose.

'Bitterly disappointed and longing only for death, I was already starting towards my arms again, for what else could I do and what alternative was open? "Were you," I said, "my own father, really expecting me to leave the house and desert you here? Could a father's lips have expressed so shocking a thought? If the Powers Above have willed that out of all this great city nothing shall remain, if your resolve is fixed, and if you mean to add the death of yourself and your kin to the ruin descending on Troy, the door to such a death stands wide open. Pyrrhus will soon be here fresh from the pool of Priam's blood, he who massacres a son before his father's eyes and then slays the father at an altar. But, O my gentle Mother, is it for this that you have been rescuing me and guarding me amid the fires and the weapons, for me to see the enemy inside my very home, and Ascanius and my father, and Creusa at their side, falling like sacrifices in one another's blood? Quick, comrades! Bring me arms. The vanquished are summoned to meet their life's end. Let me go back to the Greeks. Let me return to the battle and fight once more. We shall not all die this day unavenged!"

'Now I was buckling on my sword, slipping my left arm into the shield strap and adjusting my shield. But as I was on the point of leaving the house, there in the doorway was Creusa. She stopped me, clasping my feet and holding out our little son Iulus to his father. "If", she cried, "you go forth to die, take us also, quickly, to face with you whatever may happen. But if what you have seen of the fighting leads you to suppose that there is still any hope for us in resuming battle, your first care should be the defence of our home here. Otherwise, to whom will you leave our little Iulus, your father, and me, whom you once called your wife?"

'Loud was her appeal, and all the house was ringing with her words of anguish, when suddenly a miracle occurred. For there between the faces of the two distressed parents, and between their hands as they held him, the light cap worn by the little boy caught fire, and a bright flame, harmless to the touch, licked his soft hair, and played about his forehead. We moved quickly, trembling in alarm; we shook his hair to quench the flame, and tried to put out the holy fire with water. But my father Anchises raised his eyes to the stars in joy, and stretching his palms towards the sky said, "Jupiter Almighty, if any prayer can change your will, look down on us this once. We make one prayer only, and if our righteousness has earned some favour, give us now your presage, and confirm this sign." Scarcely had the aged prince so spoken, when with a sudden crash came thunder on the left, and a shooting star trailing a firebrand slid from the sky through the dark and darted downwards in brilliant light. Now we saw it glide above the roof of our house, sharply revealing the roads, and then, still burning bright, hide in the forests of Mount Ida. It left a long luminous streak in its wake, and far around a sulphur-smoke was seen to rise. My father was convinced. Raising himself and looking upwards he prayed to our gods and worshipped the holy star: "Ah, there is no reluctance now. I follow, Gods of our Race, and wherever you lead, there shall I be. Save our house; and save my grandson. Yours is this hallowed sign, and in your power Troy rests. And, son, for my part, I give way. I consent to go at your side."

'My father had spoken. But now through the town the roar of the fire came louder to our ears, and the rolling blaze brought its hot blast closer. "Well then, dear Father," I said, "come now, you must let them lift you onto my back. I will hold my shoulders ready for you; this labour of love will be no weight to me. Whatever chances may await us, one common peril and one salvation shall be ours. Iulus must walk beside me, and my wife shall follow at a safe distance in our footsteps. Now you others, my servants, attend to what I say. As you leave the city, there is a hillock with an ancient and deserted shrine of Ceres and by it an aged cypress-tree held in reverence by our forefathers for many years. We shall meet at this point, approaching by different routes. Now you, Father, take up the gods of our ancestral home, our holy symbols. I cannot touch them without sin, until I have washed my hands in a living spring, for coming as I do straight from the fury of war, I have fresh blood still on them." So saying, I bent down and cloaked my neck and shoulders with a red-brown lion's skin. I then took up my load. My little son Iulus twined his fingers in my right hand and kept beside his father with his short steps. Creusa followed behind. So on we went, keeping to the shadows; and now, though up till then I had remained quite unaffected by any weapons or even the sight of Greeks charging towards me, I myself was now ready to be frightened at a breath of wind and started at the slightest sound, so nervous was I, and so fearful alike for the load on my back and the companion at my side.

'I was already near the city gates and thinking that I had come all the way in safety, when suddenly we seemed to hear hurrying steps and my father, looking forward through the darkness cried, "Son, you must run for it. They are drawing near; I can see shining shields and flashes of bronze." Then, in the severe stress of my anxiety and haste, some unkind power robbed me of my wits. For after leaving the streets, which I knew, I lost direction, and I was running over trackless country when – oh, terrible! – my wife Creusa – did she stop running because some bitter fate meant to steal her from me, or did she perhaps stray from the path or just sink down in weariness? We cannot know; but we never saw her again. I had never looked back for her when she was first lost, or given her a thought till we came to the hillock consecrated to the ancient worship of Ceres. There we finally rallied all our company and found that she alone was missing, and that without knowing it her husband, her son, and her friends had lost her for ever.

'I was mad with horror; I upbraided every deity, and cursed the whole human race. In all Troy's overthrow nothing which had happened was so heartrending to me as was this loss. To my comrades I entrusted Ascanius, Anchises, and our Trojan Gods. Leaving them hidden in a winding valley I returned to Troy. I girt on again the gleaming arms. I was resolved to re-enact the whole adventure, and, exposing myself once more to every peril, to retrace my whole course through Troy.

'First I went to the shaded gateway in the city wall through which we had left, watching keenly in the darkness for my tracks and following them back. All the time I had the sense of some menacing presence and the very silence terrified me. I found my way back to our house, just in case she might have walked there, just in case. The Greeks had poured into it and now occupied the whole building. All was over; the wind rolled devouring fire high to the roof; the flames leaped over it and the hot fumes rioted to the sky. I moved on and again visited Priam's palace on the citadel. There in the deserted colonnades under Juno's protection Phoenix and the terrible Ulysses, who had been picked for the duty, kept watch over the plunder. Here the treasures pillaged from all Troy's gutted temples were being piled together, tables for divine feasts, wine-mixing bowls of solid gold, and captured garments. Children and mothers in a long, frightened line waited near. I even risked shouting through the darkness. Again and again I filled the streets with my cries in useless repetition, as in my grief I called out Creusa's name. And then, just as, distracted and with no end in sight, I was continuing my search among the city's buildings, there, directly before my eyes, appeared the very wraith of Creusa, her own mournful shade in her ghostly stature taller than life. I froze, my hair stiffened, and my voice choked in my throat. She spoke to me and her words allayed my distress: "Sweet husband, why do you allow yourself to yield to a pointless grief? What has happened is part of the divine plan. For the law of right and the Supreme Ruler of Olympus on high forbid you to carry Creusa away from Troy on your journey. You have to plough through a great waste of ocean to distant exile. And you shall come to the Western Land where the gentle current of Lydian Tiber flows between rich meadows where men are strong. There happiness and a kingdom are in store for you, with a queen for you to marry. Dispel your tears for the Creusa whom you loved. For I, being of the blood of Dardanus and a daughter to divine Venus, have not to face the arrogance of a Dolopian or Myrmidon home, or to go in slavery to women whose sons are Greeks; the Great Mother of the Gods is keeping me within the boundaries of Troyland. And now, goodbye. And guard the love of the son whom we share." Having spoken so, though I wept and longed to say so much to her, she forsook me and vanished into thin air. Three times I tried to cast my arms about her neck where she had been; but three times the clasp was in vain and the wraith escaped my hands, like airy winds, or the melting of a dream.

'With the passing of the night I returned to my comrades, and was surprised to find their number increased by a great concourse of new arrivals, mothers, husbands, and young men, all pathetically gathered together for banishment. They had come there from everywhere around with a fixed resolution, and their belongings ready, for me to lead them to any land which I might choose beyond the sea. And now the morning star was rising above the slopes near Mount Ida's crest, bringing the day. The Greeks held and blocked every entrance-gate to the city, and no hope of rescue remained. In resignation I lifted my father and moved towards the mountains.'

BOOK THREE

Ritual Sacrifice

'The Powers Above had decreed the overthrow of the Asian empire and Priam's breed of men, though they deserved a better fate. Lordly Ilium had fallen and all Neptune's Troy lay a smoking ruin on the ground. We the exiled survivors were forced by divine command to search the world for a home in some uninhabited land. So we started to build ships below Antandros, the city by the foothills of Phrygian Ida, with no idea where Destiny would take us or where we should be allowed to settle. We gathered our company together. In early summer our chieftain Anchises urged us to embark on our destined voyage. In tears I left my homeland's coast, its havens, and the plains where Troy had stood. I fared out upon the high seas, an exile with my comrades and my son, with the little Gods of our Home and the Great Gods of our race.

'Some distance from Troy is a land owned by Mars with wide plains cultivated by Thracian farmers. Once the fierce King Lycurgus had reigned there, and the country had had from of old close ties of friendship and a family alliance with Troy in the days of her prosperity. To this land I now sailed, and chose a site where the coast bends round to start on walls for our city, which I decided to call Aeneadae after my own name. But Destiny was against my enterprise.

'I was offering sacrifice to Venus the Mother and to other Deities who might favour my undertaking, and also to the Supreme King of all the Dwellers in Heaven. I was just about to sacrifice a handsome bull by the sea-shore. Quite near there happened to be a mound of earth, at the highest part of which were growing thickets of cornel and a dense cluster of spiky myrtle-stems. I went up there and tried to wrench the green growth from the ground to provide a leafy covering for our altar. There I was confronted by a horrible and astounding miracle. For from the first bush which I tried to break off at the roots from its soil, blood oozed in dark drops, fouling the earth with its spots. I felt a cold shudder run through me; my blood seemed to freeze with horror. But I persisted. Anxious to discover the cause of the mystery I tore at the resisting stalk of a second bush. But again dark blood flowed from the bark. So, greatly wondering, I began a prayer to the nymphs of the countryside and Father Mars who rules over Thracian lands, imploring them to divert the omen's dread significance and turn all to good. I tried straining with my knees against the sand and putting more weight into my efforts in a third attempt at the stems. And then – can I dare to utter it, or should my lips be sealed? – a piteous moan came from the base of the mound and I heard a human voice answering me: "Why, Aeneas, must you rend a poor sufferer? I am buried here. Wound me no more, and do not stain your righteous hands with sin. I am no foreigner: I am

Trojan-born. And when harm is done to this stalk it is human blood which flows. Ah, make haste to flee these coasts of avarice, this land of savagery! For I am Polydorus. Here death overpowered me in a crop of piercing iron-pointed spears. And so a crop resembling javelins has grown over me."

'At this my mind was crushed by uncertainty and dread. The shock stilled me; my hair stood stiff and my throat was speechless. For when the hapless Priam, realizing that Troy was condemned to a long siege, had begun to lose faith in Trojan arms, he had secretly entrusted Polydorus, and also a heavy store of gold, to the care of the King of Thrace. When Troy's power was indeed broken, and her good fortune dwindled, this king went over to the side of the victorious Agamemnon. And he broke every known law of righteousness. He murdered Polydorus and forcibly seized the gold; no wickedness is beyond a man whom that accursed gold-lust drives. When I was no longer too paralysed to move I chose some of my companions, leaders of Troy, including, of course, my father. I told them about the miracle and asked them what they thought. With one mind they insisted that we should at once leave this wicked land, break off all contact with a place which had desecrated the laws of hospitality, and let the winds bear our ships away. So we gave Polydorus a new burial, piling masses of earth on his barrow, and erecting to the Shades below an altar sad with dark drapery and the dead-black of a cypress. Ladies of Ilium, with hair duly unbound, stood by. We then offered foaming bowls of warm milk and phials of consecrated blood; and so we committed the soul to peace in its grave and lifted our voices in farewell.

'As soon as we could trust the ocean, when winds offered us smiling seas and the whisper of a breeze invited us onto the deep, my comrades crowded to the beach and launched our ships. We sailed forth from the haven, and the land and its cities sank behind us. Now far out to sea there lies Delos, a holy island with people dwelling on it, and well loved by the Nereids' Mother and Aegean Neptune. The Archer-God had found it drifting about the sea from coast to coast; and, since it was his birth-place, in loyalty to his mother, he chained it firmly to high Myconos and Gyaros; and he made it a stable dwelling-place for men, with power to scorn the waves. To Delos I now sailed, and our tired band received a safe and kindly welcome in its harbour. We disembarked and paid reverence to Apollo's city. The king was Anius, who was priest of Apollo as well as king, and wore the holy bay-leaves and ribbons on his brow. He came to meet us and recognized Anchises as an old friend. He shook hands with us, treating us as his guests; and we walked up to the palace. Reverently I entered the temple built of ancient stone and prayed: "Apollo, grant us a home of our own. We are weary. Give us a walled city which shall endure, and a lineage of our blood. Let there be some new citadel for us; henceforth preserve it as a remnant of Troy saved from the Greeks and from merciless Achilles. Who is to be our guide? Where do you bid us go, where settle our home? Be to us a father-god; tell us your will and speak direct to our hearts."

'I had scarcely spoken when of a sudden everything seemed to quake, even the God's entrance-door and his bay-tree; the whole hill on which we stood appeared to move and the shrine seemed to open and the tripod within to speak with a roar. We bowed low and fell to earth. A voice came to our ears: "O much enduring Dardans, the land of your ancestors whence you are sprung shall receive you on your return to her generous bosom. Seek out your ancient mother. And from this land the House of Aeneas, the sons of his sons, and all their descendants shall bear rule over earth's widest bounds." At Apollo's words there was a great outburst of joy and the keenest excitement. We all wondered where was the walled city which he meant when he called the wanderers to return to their ancient mother. Then my father cast his mind back over our early tradition. "Lords of Troy," he said, "hear me, and learn where your hope lies. Great Jove owns an island, Crete, set in the midst of the sea. In it there is a Mount Ida; and it is the cradle of our race. The Cretans live in a hundred great cities and the bosom of the land which they rule is fertile. And it was from Crete, if I remember rightly what I have heard, that our ancestor Teucer originally sailed to Troyland, and there chose a site for his royal capital, for until then no Ilium and no Trojan Citadel had existed there, and the people lived down in the valleys. From Crete came also the Great Mother Cybele with her ritual and her Corybants, who clash their bronze cymbals in the forests of Mount Ida; and from Crete were derived the reverential silence of our worship, and the lion-team harnessed to our Great

Lady's chariot. Now, therefore, come! Let us take the path shewn by the divine command. Let us gain the favour of the winds and sail for the realm of Cnossos. With Jupiter's help the voyage need not be long; the third dawn will see our fleet at the Cretan shores." So saying, he consecrated at the altar the proper offerings, a bull for Neptune and another for glorious Apollo, a black sheep for Storm and a white sheep for the genial West Winds.

'A rumour had rapidly spread that Idomeneus the Cretan prince had been banished from his father's kingdom, that the Cretan land was now deserted, and that we should find no enemies but only empty houses standing ready for our use. We left the harbour of Delos and sped over the seas. We threaded our way through currents racing by many shores past Naxos, where bacchanals revel on hill-slopes, past the green Isle of Reeds and the Isle of Olives, and then marble-white Paros and the Cyclades sprinkled about the sea. The shouting mariners vied with each other at their tasks. "On to Crete, the home of our forefathers!" was the cry of my friends as they urged each other on. A wind rose from astern and helped us on our way. And at length we sailed smoothly to the ancient coastlands where the Curetes dwell.

'Passionately I began work on the walls of the city for which we yearned. I called it Pergamea and my people were happy with this name. I told them that they should love their new homes and raise for our protection a high fortress. Our ships were soon nearly all high and dry on the shore, our young people already busy with weddings and work on their new farms, and I myself occupied in deciding on laws and allotting houses, when all at once, falling from some poisoned part of the sky, a heart-breaking pestilence attacked and rotted trees, crops, and men, and the only yield of that season was death. The people either lost their precious lives, or could hardly move, so ill they were. The Dog Star's heat scorched the fields till they were barren. Plants were parched and the diseased crops refused us livelihood. Then my father advised me to retrace the sea-ways to Apollo's oracle at Ortygia, and, with prayers for his indulgence, to ask him what end to our distress he would permit, where he would have us seek aid in our heavy tasks, and whither we should direct our course.

'It was night, and the creatures of the world were held in repose. But as I slept there appeared to me, standing clear before my eyes in a flood of light where the full moon poured in through windows in the walls, the divine and holy figures of our Trojan Gods which I had carried from Troy at the hour of its burning. And they spoke to me and with their words relieved my anxiety: "See, Apollo of his own will sends us to your room, and he now gives you the prophecy which he would have given you at Delian Ortygia had you sailed back there. When the fires had ruined Troyland we followed you and your arms, and in your care we traversed the heaving ocean with the fleet. And we shall exalt your grandsons to the stars and give dominion to your city. So make ready her walls, great walls for your Great Gods, and never shrink from the long effort of your exile. But you have to change your home, for Apollo of Delos never ordered you to settle in Crete, and this is not the coast which he recommended to you. There is another region for which the Greeks use the name Hesperia, the Western Land, an ancient land with might in her arms and in her fertile soil. The inhabitants used to be Oenotrians; but it is said that their descendants have now called the country Italy after one of their leaders. This Italy is our true home. From Italy came Dardanus, and Iasius, another chieftain of our blood, and founder of the Trojan nation. Come, arise! Rejoice, and hand on this message which we bring, a message true beyond doubt, to your aged father. Let him travel in quest of the Land of Italy and the town of Corythus. Jupiter denies you Mount Dicte's fields."

'At such a vision, and at the very voice of our Gods, I was bemused. This could be no dream. I seemed to recognize, there before me, their garlanded hair, and their lips as they spoke. Chill sweat spread over me. I started from my bed, raised upturned hands towards the sky with a prayer, and poured an offering of unwatered wine on the hearth. Then, glad to have performed this duty, I told Anchises exactly what had happened. Gradually he came to realize that two lines of descent from separate ancestors had been confused and that a mistake of his own had led him to misinterpret the old traditions about these lands: "O my son, you who bear the burden of Troy's destiny, nothing like this was ever foreseen by anyone except Cassandra. I remember now that one of her prophecies foretold

this destiny for our race and that she often invoked
Hesperia and Italy as our future realm, calling them by
these names. But who would ever have believed that
Trojans would travel to Hesperian shores? And who at
that time heeded Cassandra's prophecies? Let us trust
Apollo, accept his warning, and follow a better course."
So he spoke, and we were all overjoyed to obey his
instructions. We moved on from Crete as we had from
Thrace, leaving only a few of our number on the island.
We set sail and sped on our buoyant timbers across the
mighty ocean.

'When our ships were well out on the high seas,
with no longer any land in sight but on all sides nothing
but water and sky, over our heads there stood an inky-
black rain-storm, bringing tempest and gloom, and
ruffling the waters to darkness. The winds quickly set
the sea-surface rolling and lifted it in great waves. The
ships were scattered storm-tossed on the huge waste.
Clouds hid the light of day and darkness and rain
blotted out the sky; and again and again the clouds
tore apart and the lightning blazed. We were driven
off our course and wandered blindly amid the waves;
even my helmsman Palinurus said that he could not,
by looking at the sky, tell night from day, and that
in mid-ocean without landmarks he could not plan a
course. For three whole days, hard though they were
to reckon, and as many starless nights, we wandered in
the sightless murk over the ocean. [On one side the
nations of Pelops and Malea's roaring rocks hemmed
us in and land menaced us no less than the sea; and all
the time we were being battered and swamped by the

cruel waves.] Only on the fourth day did we at last gain our first sight of a coast rising before us, with distant mountains behind and smoke curling upwards. Our sails fell slack and we rose to our oars. Our oarsmen were quick to put weight into the stroke; they swept the blue surface and thrashed the sea to foam.

'Saved from the ocean I first found haven on the shores of the Strophades, in the wide Ionian sea. They are fixed now, but they are still called by this Greek name, which means the Turning Islands. They had been the home of the dreaded Celaeno and the other Harpies ever since the palace of Phineus was closed against them, and in fear of their pursuers they abandoned the tables where they had previously fed. No monster is more grim than the Harpies; no stroke of divine wrath was ever more cruel, and no wickeder demon ever soared upwards from the waters of Styx. They are birds with girls' countenances, and a disgusting outflow from their bellies. Their hands have talons and their faces are always pallid with hunger.

'Here we made the land and entered a harbour. Before us we saw prosperous herds of cattle ranging over plains, and goats unguarded on the pastures. We attacked them sword in hand, inviting the gods, including Jupiter himself, to share our plunder. Next we built seats of turf along the curving shore and started on a rich feast. But suddenly, with a terrifying swoop down from their hills and loudly flapping wings, the Harpies were upon us. They pillaged our meal, making everything filthy with their unclean touch; their stench was foul and their screams horrible. Then once more we laid out our tables and relighted the altar fire, this time in a deep retreat under an overhanging rock [and enclosed by trees which cast a mysterious shade]. But the noisy flock, which had been hiding out of sight, swooped down on us from a different point, flew round the prey with their clawed feet, and again fouled the food with their lips. I immediately gave my orders to my comrades: they must take up arms for we had to make war on this grotesque tribe. They did exactly as I bade them, concealing their swords here and there in the grass and placing their shields out of sight. Accordingly, when the Harpies swooped clattering down over the curving beach, Misenus from a point of vantage sounded the alarm on his bronze trumpet. At the sound my comrades charged, and attempted a weird battle, seeking to inflict sword-wounds on these sinister, filthy ocean-birds. But they did not feel our blows on their feathers and no wound ever reached the skin on their backs; they fled swiftly, soaring to the sky and leaving behind them the remains of the meal and the revolting traces of their visit. But now one of them, Celaeno herself, perching high on a rock, broke silence and spoke to us like a prophetess of doom: "So, you kindred of Laomedon, so you would go to war to defend your cattle-raiding? You would fight for these slaughtered bullocks? And drive us innocent Harpies from our rightful realm? Attend then to my words and fix them in your thoughts. For I, chief among all Furies, reveal to you a prophecy which Phoebus Apollo made to me, having himself received it from the Father, the Almighty. Italy is the destination of your voyage. You will invite the winds, and to Italy you will go. You will not be forbidden to enter an Italian harbour. But never shall you be granted a city, to gird it with your walls, until first, to punish you for your sin in striking at us, a fearful hunger has forced you to gnaw and devour your very tables." With these words she flew away and darted swiftly back into the wood.

'At this my comrades' blood chilled and froze in sudden dread. Their spirits sank and they advised me to rely for our deliverance not on weapons but on prayers and vows, whether the Harpies were goddesses or only sinister, filthy birds. My father Anchises, standing on the beach, stretched forth his opened hands and called upon the High Powers. He appointed for us the required rites of worship, and prayed: "Gods, forfend this menace and avert all such calamities. Be gracious, and preserve righteous men." Next he commanded us to fling hawsers from moorings and uncoil and ease the sheets. South winds stretched our sails. We fled over foaming waves where the wind, and the helmsman, chose us a course. And now the wave-girt wooded island of Zacynthus came into view, and then Dulichium, Same, and Neritos with its steep stone cliffs. We evaded the rocks of Ithaca where Laertes had reigned, and cursed the land which had given birth to the savage Ulysses. Presently there appeared before us the cloud-capped headland of Leucate, and Apollo's temple on the mainland promontory which seafarers hold in dread. Being weary, we put in to land and cast anchors from the prows. The sterns made a line along the beach. We walked up to the little city.

'So, beyond all our hopes, we had at last won our way to land. We cleansed ourselves ritually in Jupiter's sight and kindled altars whereon to repay our vows. Next we held Trojan games on the shore of Actium, and great was the throng. My comrades stripped themselves and sleek with olive oil engaged in their sports just as on the wrestling-grounds of their old home, happy to think that they had safely escaped their enemies and kept clear of so many Greek cities on their way. Meanwhile the sun in his annual course round the year rolled on. Ice came, the winter's north wind roughened the waves of the sea. I fixed on a door-frontal a shield of hollowed bronze which had once been carried by the mighty Abas, and under it wrote a memorial, "Armour captured from victorious Greeks and dedicated by Aeneas". Then I gave the order to man the rowing-seats and leave port. My comrades swept the sea-surface, striking it in rivalry. Very soon we saw Phaeacia's airy heights sink behind us, and skirted the shores of Epirus till we approached the harbour of Chaonia and finally reached the hill-city of Buthrotum.

'Here we heard a strange tale, almost beyond belief. Helenus, Priam's son, had been accepted as a king among Greeks. He had succeeded to the throne of Pyrrhus the Aeacid and had married his queen Andromache, who thus became united once more to a husband of her own kin. I was struck with amazement, and in rare curiosity hurried to question Helenus and hear more of this extraordinary outcome. I left the shore and my ships and was walking up from the harbour when I chanced on Andromache herself, sorrowfully pouring a drink offering in a ritual of sacrifice to Hector's ashes. In a wood near her city by a river named after the Simois she was calling on Hector's spirit at his cenotaph of green turf, where she had reverently set up two altars as a place for her mourning. Andromache was aghast to see me approaching, equipped as I was in Trojan style. Unnerved by the shock, suddenly, as she looked, she stiffened; the warmth left her, she could hardly stand, and it was some time before she could find words: "Are you real? Can I believe my eyes? Son of the Goddess, may I know that it is you? Are you a living man? Or, if life's light has passed from you, tell me, where is Hector?" As she spoke she broke into tears and the whole place was loud with her crying. So wild was her grief that I was only able to interrupt with short answers, following at intervals as best they could: "Yes, I am indeed a living man; life goes on for me, but in keenest suffering. Have no doubts; your eyes do not deceive you. But, oh, what has fate done to you since you fell from the high estate of your illustrious marriage? Has fortune smiled on you again, as brightly as Hector's Andromache deserves? Are you still the wife of Pyrrhus?"

'She replied, speaking low and with downcast face: "Ah, happy beyond all others is that daughter of Priam who was sentenced to die by an enemy's grave at the foot of Troy's towering ramparts! She was no captive slave, chosen by lot to gratify a conqueror's lust. I saw my home burnt. I was carried far across the seas to suffer the scornful arrogance of Achilles' young son, and endured all the travail of slavery. However, my husband soon left me, being passionately eager to marry a Spartan named Hermione, the grand-daughter of Leda, and so passed me on to be mate to Helenus, two house-slaves together. Meanwhile, Orestes, who was still being tormented by the Furies for his crime, and whose wife it was that Pyrrhus now planned to steal, burning with jealousy lay in wait for Pyrrhus, caught him off guard, and stabbed him to death at the altar of his home. After Pyrrhus died, part of his realm passed to Helenus in course of law. He chose the names Chaonia and the Chaonian Plain after Chaon in Troyland, and built above the hill-slopes a Fortress of Ilium, a Citadel of Troy. But you, what winds and what destiny have brought you voyaging here? Or perhaps some God forced you to land, in ignorance, upon our shores? What of your little son, Ascanius? Does he still live, and still breathe the strengthening air? You had him with you in Troy . . . And can he remember the mother whom he lost? Does he know that Aeneas is his father and Hector was his uncle, and does the knowledge already awake in him the qualities of a man and the spirit of olden time?"

'She was still asking me this torrent of questions, and weeping and moaning with long, vain sobs, when Priam's princely son, Helenus himself, came walking from the city walls with a large retinue. He recognized his kin with joy and led us to the gate, talking to us with many tears at every word. As I walked onwards I recognized this little "Troy", with its citadel built to resemble the old citadel, and a dry water-course called

"Xanthus"; and I even saluted the threshold of a "Scaean Gate".

'The other Trojans gladly joined me in sharing the city's friendship. The king received them in a spacious colonnade. In a courtyard a meal on gold plate was set, and from bowls in their hands they poured an offering of the gift of Bacchus.

'And now day followed day, and breezes invited our sails; a south wind was filling and swelling the canvas. Therefore I spoke to Helenus, who had the power of prophecy, and asked him questions: "You, Trojan-born, are Heaven's interpreter. You know the truth of Apollo's power, you know his tripods, his bay-trees at Claros, the stars too and the voices of birds, and the prophetic meanings of their flight. Come, speak to me. My every pious observance has given me fair hope for my voyaging. Every divine message has urged me, with its whole authority, to force my way onwards towards distant lands and sail for Italy, except only Celaeno the Harpy who pronounced against me grim wrath to come and prophesied a monstrous event, a blasphemy even to mention, a famine meaning doom. Therefore, what dangers shall I principally avoid? What will guide me safely through the dread ordeals to come?"

'At this Helenus first formally sacrificed bullocks, and won the gods' indulgence with a prayer. He next relaxed the ribbon round his hallowed head, and in high fervour, so strong was the divine power, he led me by the hand to Phoebus Apollo's door. Then, straightway, by right of priesthood from inspired lips he prophesied: "Son of the Goddess, it is clear and it

is certain that you traverse the deep by sanctions from
the Greater Powers. So are the lots of destiny drawn
by the King of Gods; so does he set events to roll their
course; so does he turn the pages of history to come. I
shall speak, in my words to you, out of many truths
a few only, that you may voyage the more safely
over foreign seas and succeed in reaching repose in an
Italian harbour. For the rest, either the Fates allow
not Helenus to know, or Saturnian Juno forbids his
prophesying. First, therefore, you have been ignorantly
assuming that Italy is now near enough for you to sail
direct to one of its havens. But for you Italy is still far,
and lies at the end of a long voyage over uncharted
waters and past long coastlands. And you must first
strain at the oar in Sicilian waters, your ships must
traverse the salt surface of the Italian seas, and you
must pass by the Infernal Lakes and Circe's Aeaean
Isle before you can settle your city on safe soil. Now I
shall give you a sign; store it in your thoughts, and
remember. When in an anxious time you shall find
lying by a distant river's water under holm-oak trees
on the bank a huge white sow, stretched on the ground
with her thirty young which she has just farrowed, all
white like her, gathered round her teats, that place
shall be the site for your city, and there you shall find
sure repose from your tribulations. And be not appalled
by the fear of gnawing your tables; Destiny will find a
way for you, and if you call on him Apollo will be there
to aid. But you must avoid the land on this side, along
the nearer coastline of Italy, which is closer to us than
any other shore washed by our own sea's tide, for there

every walled city contains hostile Greeks. One of these cities was founded by Locrians of Narycium. In another is Idomeneus of Crete, whose men-at-arms infest the level lands of the Sallentinians. Elsewhere is little Petelia, the famous town of Philoctetes the chieftain from Meliboea; it seems to rest on its encircling wall. But, when you have passed them all, and your fleet rides in safety on the sea's farther side, then must you erect altars on the beach and repay your vows. When you do so you must be clothed in purple raiment, which shall even veil your hair, lest, while you are at worship and the hallowed fires are burning, some intruder's presence may obscure the divine message. Your comrades as well as yourself must always observe this rule of sacrifice, and your descendants, if they would be pure of conscience, must stay faithful to this rite.

'"Now further, when you have departed thence, the wind will carry you near the coast of Sicily and the barriers of narrow Pelorus will open to show a clear passage. Then you must steer for the land on your port side, sailing in that direction on a long, circuitous course over the open water, and avoiding the shore and the sea to starboard. It is said that the lands here were in the past one unbroken whole, but that some titanic convulsion long since tore them up so that they flew apart, for time's vast antiquity has been sufficient to compass even so mighty a change. And next the sea burst violently between, rent the Italian cities apart from Sicily's coast, and flowed in its narrow mill-race severing the lands and the cities which their new coast-lines sundered. Here your way will be blocked by Scylla on the right and on the left by the never-pacified Charybdis, who thrice in a day drinks giant waves down the sheer depth of her engulfing abyss, and then shoots them up again to the sky, as though trying to lash the stars with water. Scylla however hides in a cavern and remains out of sight; but she thrusts out her mouths and sucks ships onto the rocks. Her upper half, as far as the groin, is human in shape as of a maid with a fair breast, but her lower part is a monstrous whale with many dolphin-tails growing from wolves' bellies. It will be wiser not to hasten but rather to take a long and roundabout course, bending back again at Cape Pachynus in Sicily, than to risk setting eyes even once on the hideous Scylla deep in her monstrous cavern, where the rocks are loud with the bark of her sea-blue hounds. And more: so surely as Helenus has second sight, and his prophecy deserves belief, so surely as Apollo inspires him with truth, even so, O Goddess-Born, I will pronounce to you one supreme duty, in itself as peremptory and important as all the rest together, and I would repeat this warning again and again and again. Above all you shall worship mighty Juno's godhead and offer her entreaties; and with your whole will submit your vows to her. And you shall win that mighty Mistress over to you by offerings in supplication; for only so may you leave Sicily behind you and come victoriously to Italy's frontier. Then, having reached Italy, you shall first visit the city of Cumae where lie ghostly lakes amid Avernus' whispering forests. There shall you see a frantic maiden-prophetess who from deep within a cavern of rock foretells the decrees of Destiny. She commits words to writing by making marks on leaves; afterwards she sorts into order all the prophecies which she has written on them, and allows their messages to remain, a closed secret, in her cave. There they stay, all in order and motionless; but if once the hinge-post turns and even a slight wind strikes them, the delicate leaves are disturbed by the door's movement, and the prophetess never afterwards thinks of catching them as they flit within the rock-hollow, or of putting them together again into prophecies. Consultants therefore depart unanswered, and are bitter against the sibyl's oracle. Now, to save you from so costly a loss of time, I warn you that however your comrades chide you, and even though your plan for your voyage urgently invites your sails onto the deep with a following wind to fill your bellying canvas, you must nevertheless visit the prophetess, and with insistent entreaty extort responses from her; you must make her unseal her lips and pronounce her answers herself with her own speech. She will then reveal to you the nations of Italy, the wars which you must fight, and how you may escape or endure each of the ordeals to come. If you court her well, she will give you a fair passage.

'"These, then, are the directions which, in answer to your wish, my lips are permitted to give to you. Therefore go forth, and by your deeds exalt our Troy in grandeur to the skies."

'Having spoken his prophecy, the kindly seer next gave orders for gifts to be conveyed to our ships, heavy objects of gold and wrought ivory. He packed into the holds a large store of silver, cauldrons from Dodona, and a corslet of hooked chain-mail and three-leash golden weave, and a splendid helmet, coned and crested with long hair, both once owned by Pyrrhus. There were special gifts for my father. Helenus also provided us with horses and with guides. He rearmed my company, and gave us more oarsmen to complete our crews.

'While Helenus was so engaged, Anchises had been commanding us to bend sails onto spars, to make sure that we should not be late in using any favouring wind. And now Helenus, Apollo's own spokesman, addressed Anchises with profound respect: "Anchises, counted fit for exalted marriage with Venus herself, Anchises for whom Gods take thought since twice have they saved you from falling Troy, see – Italy's land is before you, sail fast, and make it yours. But first you must voyage right on, coasting along the nearer side of Italy, which lies out there, across the sea, for it is the far side of Italy which Apollo unlocks for you. Go forth in the strength of your son's loyalty, But why do I continue so? The winds are rising. I must not keep them waiting by my talk."

'And Andromache, too, sad indeed now that the moment for parting had come, was no less generous, and did not lag behind in her liberality. She brought for Ascanius figured garments with woof-thread of gold and an embroidered mantle from Troy. As she loaded him with the woven gifts she spoke to him: "Ascanius, dear, do take these gifts as well; they are from me, to remind you of my handiwork, and to be a

lasting token that Hector's Andromache always loves
you. Take them, the last gifts to you from your own
kin, for all that is left to me of my Astyanax is his
likeness in you. His eyes, his hands, his face and his
movements were just like yours; and he would now
have grown to be just your age."

'As I left them, with tears welling, I spoke: "Live,
and prosper, for all your adventures are past. We are
called ever onwards from destiny to destiny. For you,
your rest is won. You have no expanse of sea to plough,
no land of Italy, seeming always to recede before you,
as your quest. You may look at your copy of the river
Xanthus, and at a Troy built by your own hands, with
fairer prospects, I hope, and no more fear of danger
from the Greeks. And if I ever reach Tiber's estuary,
stand beside it on its fields, and see those city-walls
which have been promised to my people, then one day
in Italy we shall create by our mutual sympathy kindred
cities having close ties with Epirus, a Western Land
sharing one founder, Dardanus, and one same history
with you; and you and we shall be each equally a Troy.
May this be a duty for our descendants to inherit!"

'We sailed out to sea close to the nearby Ceraunian
headland, whence the passage by water to Italy is the
shortest. As we passed, the sun sank, and the moun-
tains were shadowed in darkness. We disembarked,
and, drawing lots for turns on watch by the oars, we
thankfully stretched ourselves on the kindly earth close
by the sea. So we lay scattered about the dry beach and
refreshed ourselves. Sleep came to strengthen our tired
limbs. But Night, sped by the hours, was not yet near-

ing the mid point of her cycle when the ever-alert
Palinurus left his couch and listened intently for a
wind, caring little from what quarter it might come;
he checked every constellation which glided solemnly
over the voiceless heaven, Arcturus, the Hyads which
foretell the rain, and the Two Bears, and then, as his
eyes roved, Orion of the golden sword. Next, seeing
that all was calm and the sky serene, he stood on his
ship's stern and sounded a sharp call. We struck camp,
adventured out on our way, and spread the wings of
our sails. And now, when dawn with its first red glow
had routed the stars, we could just see hills along a low
coastline across the waters. "Italy!" Achates was the
first to shout the name. "Italy!" cried my comrades in
joyful welcome. Anchises my father standing high on
the quarter-deck took a large wine-bowl, wreathed it,
filled it with unwatered wine, and invoked our Gods:
"Gods of the Earth, Gods of the Sea, Gods who have
rule over storms, give us a wind to help our voyage,
and may your breath bring us aid."

'Quicker now came the breeze in answer to his
prayer. Quite near, a harbour opened ahead of us; and
Minerva's Temple, on the height, came into view. My
comrades furled their sails and swung our prows
towards land. The harbour had been formed into the
shape of a bent bow by waves blown from the east. It
was hidden by projecting rocks which foamed with salt
spray, and from the towered crags its two walls, like
drooping arms, ran steeply down. The temple lay back
from the shore. And here I saw our first prophetic sign,
four shining snow-white horses straying and cropping

the grass on the plain. My father Anchises exclaimed, "War, O Stranger Land, is the message which you bring us; horses are equipped for war, and it is war that these animals threaten. Yet there are times when these same four-foot creatures are trained for harnessing in a team and are yoked in harmony and bridled in contentment." And he added, "So there is also a hope of peace." Then we offered prayers to the holy might of weapon-clashing Minerva who was the first to welcome our exultant band. We stood before the altars, our heads veiled with Phrygian cloth; and in due form kindled the sacrifice to Argive Juno which Helenus had warned us to remember as the most momentous of his commands. We did not wait; having duly performed our vows we immediately swung to the wind our yard-arms and our sails; and so we left those fields, not trusting any place where men of Greek stock dwelt. Our next sight was Tarentum on its gulf, a city visited, if the tale is true, by Hercules; and opposite to it towered Lacinian Juno's temple. Yes, and there stood Caulonia's fortress, and there Scylaceum, where ships founder. And now far off, and rising from the sea, Sicilian Etna was visible, and we heard in the distance the ocean's mighty waves crashing on rocks, and loud and fitful sounds audible alongshore. Sea-water spurted from the depths, and sand swirled in the boiling surge. My father Anchises cried, "This must surely be the dreaded Charybdis; those terrifying rocks, there, are the crags of which Helenus warned us. Tear yourselves free. Jump to your oars, and keep together." My comrades did as they were commanded. Palinurus was the

first to wrench his roaring prow to port and out to sea;
then all our company made after him with oars and
sails. We were lifted towards the sky on a heaving
swell, but again the waves drew off, and all at once we
were settling deep down, and sinking towards Hades.
Three times the crags shouted the echo of the sea back
at us as we lay wallowing low between arching rocks.
Three times we looked through foam spewed from the
sea and saw the sky through a screen of spray. But
meanwhile both wind and sunlight had deserted us.
We were tired, and, not knowing our way, we gently
drifted to the coast of the Cyclopes.

'The harbour there is spacious enough, and calm,
for no winds reach it, but close by Etna thunders and
its affrighting showers fall. Sometimes it ejects up to
high heaven a cloud of utter black, bursting forth in a
tornado of pitchy smoke with white-hot lava, and
shoots tongues of flame to lick the stars. Sometimes
the mountain tears out the rocks which are its entrails
and hurls them upwards. Loud is the roar each time
the pit in its depth boils over, and condenses this
molten stone and hoists it high in the air. The story is
told that huge Enceladus, whom the bolt of thunder
charred, lies crushed under Etna's mass and that the
enormous volcano stands there above him, breathing
flames from its bursting furnaces; and, each time that
Enceladus tires and turns over, all Sicily quakes and
growls and veils the sky with smoke. All that night
we hid in the forest subjected to fantastic experiences
without seeing what caused the noise. There were no
blazing constellations, no height of heaven bright with

a starry glow, but only mists in a muffled sky and the moon wrapped in murk at deadest night.

'And now the morrow was arising with a first gleam in the east, and already the sunrise had parted the moist shadows from high heaven, when suddenly there emerged from the forest a grotesque stranger, pitifully unkempt and gaunt with starvation. He stretched his hands in entreaty to us on the shore. We looked at him with curiosity. His dirt was fearful, his beard untended, and his garment hooked together with thorns. But in all else he was a Greek, who had once gone on the expedition to Troy wearing his father's arms. When he saw before him Dardan dress and Trojan weapons, he checked his walk, stood for a moment frozen in terror, and then dashed headlong to the beach with tears and entreaties: "I implore you, Trojans, by the stars, by the High Gods, by the shining air which is our breath, carry me away, take me to any land which you choose; that is all I wish. I know that I was a member of the Greek expedition. I confess that I made war on Trojan homes. For that, if the dreadful wrong caused by my crime deserves it, scatter me in fragments over the waves and drown me in the wastes of sea. If I must die, death by a human hand will be happiness."

'With this cry, he clasped my knees and clung to them grovelling. We encouraged him to tell us who he was and of what breed, and to recount his sufferings at the hands of fortune. After a little pause my father Anchises gave his hand to the young stranger, increasing his confidence by this willing gesture, so that at last he laid his dread aside and spoke:

'"I come from Ithaca, which was my home, and I was a comrade of the ill-fated Ulysses. My name is Achaemenides and my father was Adamastus. He was a poor man; and how I wish we had stayed as we were! But I parted from him, and I sailed for Troy. I was left here in the Cyclops' monstrous cave by my comrades, who forgot me in their pressing anxiety to escape through that horrible entrance. The interior of the dwelling is dark and enormous, and filthy too from those bloody meals. The Cyclops is a giant, towering high enough to hit the sky; oh, Gods, fend such a horror far from the world of men! He is an offence to our eyes, and not to be addressed in human converse by any man. He feeds on the inner parts and dark blood of his poor victims. I myself have seen him grasp two of our number in that huge hand, and, still lying prone in the centre of his cave, smash them on a rock; I have seen all the passage-way splashed and swimming with gore. I have seen him chew their limbs, all dripping and blackened with clotting blood, and their joints quiver, still warm, as his jaws closed. But he suffered for his deed. Ulysses could not let such savagery pass; and in this grim crisis our Ithacan proved true to himself. For no sooner was the Cyclops replete with his eating and sunk in a drunken sleep, stretched vast across his cave with his neck bent and vomiting, as he slept, morsels of food, thick wine, and blood mixed together with other filth, when we, with a prayer to the High Powers, drew lots for our tasks. Together, we all dashed in to surround him. With a sharp instrument we pierced the huge single eye set deep below his frowning forehead and as big as an Argive shield or Apollo's sun; and gleefully we avenged the ghosts of our comrades. But you, you poor strangers, you must hasten to escape. Rend your hawsers from the shore. There are a hundred other appalling Cyclopes, just like this Polyphemus who pens and milks his woolly flock in his spacious cave, and just as large, living everywhere on the coastland along this curving shore and straying high up into the mountains. For the third time now the moon is filling her horns with light, and for so long have I been dragging out my days in the woods and the wilderness where only beasts have their haunts and lairs, observing these fearful Cyclopes from a rock on which I used to stand and ready to start trembling at every sound of their feet and voices. I have been living on meagre fare from the boughs; stony cornel-berries and grasses torn up from their roots have been my food. And, though I was always on the look-out, never till now have I caught sight of any ships sailing to this coast. When I saw yours, I decided to trust myself entirely to them, whatever they might be, for surely nothing could matter if once I escaped from the appalling race of Cyclopes. Rather than face them I would let you end my life by any means you choose."

'He had scarcely finished when we saw Polyphemus himself, massive and monstrous, walking down from the mountain-heights with his flock about him, which he was shepherding as usual to the sea-shore, a horrible and hideous ogre of a giant with his eyesight gone. He carried a pine-trunk cut short, to guide his hand and steady his steps; the fleecy ewes which went with him were his sole joy and now his only consolation. And then he waded out into the sea until he reached deep water. Groaning and grinding his teeth he washed off the blood which flowed where his gouged eye had been. He walked on now far out from land, but still the waves never wetted his towering thighs. In alarm we took on board the suppliant, who had earned his rescue; we cut our cables in silence, and hastened to escape beyond the Cyclops' reach. We bent to it and competing with each other churned the sea-surface with our oars. The Cyclops suspected something and turned his footsteps towards the sounds. But since he had no way of aiming a cast at us, nor, if he pursued, was he tall enough to wade in the waves of the Ionian Sea, he raised a tremendous shout. At that shout every ripple of the ocean trembled, far inland the country of Italy took fright, and even Etna bellowed from the depths of its winding subterranean caverns. And now the whole tribe of Cyclopes was aroused. They dashed to the harbour from forest and mountain height, and thronged the shore. We could see them standing there, that brotherhood of Etna, helpless for all their grim eyes and heads towering to the sky; a horrifying assembly, like so many oak-trees growing in Jupiter's forest on mountain-crests and lifting heads high in air; or like a group of cypress-conifers in Diana's stately grove. Our sharp terror urged us to shake our sheets free and stretch our sails to the following winds in headlong flight, regardless of its direction. But Helenus had given a very different counsel, not to steer between Scylla and Charybdis, since the passage between them came within a narrow margin of disaster on either hand. So we decided to trim our canvas and put back. But then a north wind suddenly arose, blowing over the narrow headland of Pelorus. We sailed carefully past the river Pantagia's harbour-mouth, formed of natural rock, past Megara's bay, and low-lying Thapsus. Achaemenides gave me information about these places, recalling in the reverse order his memories of the shores which he had passed in his wanderings as a shipmate of the luckless Ulysses.

'Plemmyrium, with its flooding waves, called Ortygia by earlier men, lies stretched in front of the Sicanian Bay. A story tells how Alpheus the river of Elis forced his unseen way below the sea to mingle with Sicilian waters at the mouth of Arethusa's stream. There, in obedience to the command, we paid reverence to the High Powers. Next we passed beyond Helorus, the marsh-city of rich soil. After that we sailed by the projecting rocks and reefs of Pachynus. Then into view came Camarina, which according to the oracle "might never be moved", and after it Gela's plains and Gela itself, cruel city called after the name of a laughing river. Next the steep Acragas, once a breeding ground for horses of highest mettle, displayed before us its mighty ramparts. The winds were kindly; I left leafy Selinus behind and picked my way by Lilybaeum through the difficult shallows with their hidden rocks. At last I found a harbour at Drepanum, but there was no joy for me on that shore. For here, after all the persecution of the ocean-storms, O bitterness! I lost my father, lost Anchises, my solace in every adventure and every care. Yes, here, in my weary plight, you, best of fathers, forsook me, after I had brought you so far and through so many dire perils in vain. Even Helenus the seer never foretold this grief to me among all his many dread warnings, nor did foul Celaeno. This blow was my last anguish. For I had reached the destination of my voyage; and I was sailing from Sicily when Providence drove me onto your coast.'

So did Troy's chieftain Aeneas recall his tale of divine destiny and describe his voyaging, with each face turned intently towards him. At last he ceased; here he fell silent, his story at an end.

BOOK FOUR
The Tragedy of Dido

But meanwhile Queen Dido, gnawed by love's invisible fire, had long suffered from the deep wound draining her life-blood. Again and again the thought of her hero's valour and the high nobility of his descent came forcibly back to her, and his countenance and his words stayed imprinted on her mind; the distress allowed her no peace and no rest. And now the next day's dawn was cleansing the world with Apollo's light and had parted the moist shadows in high heaven, when Dido spoke distractedly to the sister whose heart was one with hers: 'Anna, Sister Anna, why am I poised frightened between fitful sleep and waking? What do you think of this new guest who has joined us in our home? He has a rare presence, and valiant indeed are his heart and his arms. I can well believe, and I have a right to believe, that his parentage is divine. An ignoble spirit is always revealed by fear. But – what torments from destiny and what horrors of war, endured to the bitterest end, were in his story! If I had not been irrevocably resolved never again to desire a union in wedlock with any man, since the time when death's treachery cheated me of my first love, and if all thought of the marriage-rite and the bridalroom had not become utter weariness

to me, possibly this might have been the one tempta-
tion to which I could have fallen. Yes, Anna, I shall
tell you my secret. Ever since the tragic death of my
husband Sychaeus, whose sprinkled blood, which my
own brother shed, desecrated our home, no one but
this stranger ever made an impression on me, or stirred
my heart to wavering. I can discern the old fire coming
near again. But I could pray that the earth should yawn
deep to engulf me, or the Father Almighty blast me to
the Shades with a stroke of his thunder, deep down to
those pallid Shades in darkest Erebos, before ever I
violate my honour or break its laws. For he who first
united me with him took all love out of my life; and
so it is he who should keep it close to his heart and
guard it even in the grave.' She had spoken her
thoughts; and the tears welled, and wetted the fold of
her garment which she held to her eyes.

Anna answered her: 'Sister mine, whom I love more
than life itself, will you live alone sorrowing and pining
through all your youth, and never know the love of
children and all that Venus gives? Do you really believe
that this matters to ashes, to a ghost in a grave? Granted
that in the past no African nor, before we came here,
any Tyrian suitor could ever tempt you from your grief,
for you scorned Iarbas and other chieftains, sons of
this land so fertile in victorious fame; must you there-
fore now resist a love which appeals to you? Besides,
you should remember who are the owners of the land
in which is your settlement. You are hemmed in on
one side of you by the cities of the unconquerable
Gaetulians, by Numidians who know no curb, and by

the forbidding quicksands, the Syrtes, and on the other by a waterless desert and the ferocious raiders from Barca. And I need not speak of the danger of war from Tyre, where your brother continues his threats. Now it is my belief that, when these Trojan ships kept course for Carthage before the wind, the gods themselves sealed their approval and Juno herself gave her support. And, Dido, only imagine, if you make this splendid marriage, what a great future lies in store for our city and our realm! With a Trojan army marching at our side, think what deeds of prowess will exalt the fame of Carthage! You have only to pray to the gods for their blessing and ensure their favour by sacrifice; and then entertain your guest freely, weaving pretexts for keeping him here, while his ships are still damaged, and winter and Orion the rain-bringer spend their fury on the ocean under a forbidding sky.'

By speaking so Anna set Dido's heart, already kindled, ablaze with a new access of love, gave new hope to tempt her wavering intention, and broke down her scruples. Their first act was to visit the shrines and pray to the gods for their indulgence at each altar in turn, formally sacrificing selected sheep to Ceres the Mistress of Increase, to Phoebus, to Father Bacchus the Freedom-Giver, and above all to Juno, for the tie of marriage lies in her care. Lovely Dido herself would take the bowl in her right hand and pour the wine between the horns of a pure white cow, or she would pace in the ritual dance near the gods' reeking altars before the eyes of their statues. She would present more victims to start the day of service anew, and peer with parted lips into the open breasts of sheep for the message of their still breathing vitals. But how pitifully weak is the prescience of seers! There lay no help for her infatuation in temples or in prayers; for all the time the flame ate into her melting marrow, and deep in her heart the wound was silently alive. Poor Dido was afire, and roamed distraught all over her city; like a doe caught off her guard and pierced by an arrow from some armed shepherd, who from the distance had chased her amid Cretan woods and without knowing it had left in her his winged barb; so that she traverses in her flight forests and mountain tracks on Dicte, with the deadly reed fast in her flesh. Sometimes Dido would take Aeneas where her walls were being built, letting him see the great resources of Phoenicia and how far the construction of her city had progressed. And she would begin to speak her thoughts, but always check herself with the words half-spoken. At day's decline she would want the banqueting to begin again as before; she would insist beyond all reason on hearing yet once more the tale of Troy's anguish, and again she would hang breathless on the speaker's words. Afterwards, when they had parted, as the moon in her turn quenched her light to darkness and the setting stars counselled sleep, Dido mourned, lonely in the empty banqueting-hall, and threw herself on the couch which he had left. He was away now, out of sight and hearing, but she still saw him and still heard his voice. Sometimes she held Ascanius close to her, under the spell of his resemblance to his father, and trying hard to escape from the love which she dared not tell.

Meanwhile the partly built towers had ceased to rise. No more did young soldiers practise arms. The construction of harbours and impregnable battlements came to a stop. Work hung suspended on gigantic, menacing walls, and the sky-high cranes were still.

Now no sooner had Saturn's daughter, Jupiter's dear wife, seen that Dido was in the firm grip of her affliction and that no thought of her reputation any longer resisted her passion, than she approached Venus with a suggestion: 'Well, you and that boy of yours certainly have fine fruits of victory to show, and great is the glory which you have won. Your distinction is indeed high and deserves to be famous, now that you two divinities have managed to trick one woman into defeat. At the same time I am not wholly unaware that you only view the peaceful homes of tall Carthage with suspicion because you fear the strength of my city's defences. But how far do you mean to go? What need is there to continue so fierce a rivalry? Surely it is better for us to collaborate in arranging a permanent peace, sealed by a marriage-compact. You have gained the object on which you had set your heart. Dido has drunk the maddening poison into her very bones; she is ablaze with love. Let us therefore share this nation between us, each having equal authority in its government. Let Dido be free to become a Phrygian's slave-wife and to hand over her Tyrians into your power as the dowry.'

But Venus realized that Juno's words did not express her true purpose and that her real intention was to divert to Africa those who were meant by Destiny to hold rule in Italy. So this is how she replied: 'Ah, who indeed would be so mad as to refuse such an offer, at the cost of being matched against you in war? Provided, of course, that the plan which you describe will, when put in practice, be crowned with success. But I am subject to the Fates, whose design is obscure to me. Would Jupiter wish the Tyrians and the emigrants from Troy to own a city in common, and would he approve of a treaty between them, or any blending of populations? Now you are his wife; there is nothing wrong in your exploring his intentions by a direct request. So go forward; I shall follow.'

Queenly Juno had a reply to make: 'That task will be my responsibility. But now let me briefly explain how we may achieve our immediate purpose. Listen. As soon as tomorrow's sun rises at the dawning to unveil the earth with his rays, Aeneas and the hapless Dido mean to go hunting in a forest together. While the beaters are hurrying to stretch their encircling cordons across the mountain-tracks, I shall set over them a black cloud charged with mingled rain and hail, release a downpour on the royal pair, and awake all the sky with thunder. Their retinue will scatter and vanish in a darkness as of night, and Dido and Troy's chieftain will both take shelter in the same cave. I shall be there, and if I may be sure of your compliance, I shall assign her to him to be his own, and unite them in secure marriage. This shall be their lawful wedding.' To this proposal the Cytherean raised no objection. She nodded her assent, with a smile at so ingenious a deception.

Meanwhile Aurora arose and left the ocean. When

her rays appeared, a select company issued from the city-gates. Out came the wide-meshed nets, the small stop-nets, and the hunting spears with their broad iron heads; and out dashed Massylian riders, and a pack of keen-scented hounds. The queen still lingered in her own room, while the noblest among the Carthaginians awaited her at the doors. Her spirited horse, caparisoned in a splendour of purple and gold, pawed the ground and champed a foaming bit. At last she came, stepping forth with a numerous suite around her and clad in a Sidonian mantle with an embroidered hem. Golden was her quiver and the clasp which knotted her hair, and golden was the brooch which fastened the purple tunic at her neck. Up came the Trojan party, too, including the delighted Iulus. As the two processions met, Aeneas, by far the most handsome of them all, passed across to Dido's side. He was like Apollo when in winter he leaves Lycia and the river Xanthus and visits his mother's isle Delos to start the dancing anew, while around his altar, Cretans, Dryopians and tattooed Agathyrsans mingle and cheer; Apollo himself paces on the slopes of Cynthus, with his clattering bow and arrows slung from his shoulder and his flowing hair pressed into neatness by a soft wreath of leaves and held by a band of gold. Aeneas walked as alertly as he; and a grace like Apollo's shone from his noble face.

When the hunters had reached a pathless tract high in the hills, they started a flock of wild goats which came galloping down the slopes from a rocky crest straight in front of them; and, farther round, a herd of stags massed their ranks in a cloud of dust and fled away from the hill-country and across the open moors. Deep in the valley below, the young Ascanius was keenly enjoying his ride on a spirited horse, out-stripping now these and now those at full gallop; but how he longed to see appearing among all these harm-less creatures a boar, mouth a-foam, or a golden-brown lion, prowling down from the hills!

Soon a confused rumbling sound started in the sky. Then came the rain-clouds and showers mixed with hail. The hunters all scattered in alarm about the fields searching for shelter – the Tyrian retinue, the band of young Trojans, and the Dardan boy who was grandson of Venus. Torrents came streaming from the hills. Dido and Troy's chieftain found their way to the same cavern. Primaeval Earth and Juno, Mistress of the Marriage, gave their sign. The sky connived at the union; the lightning flared; on their mountain-peak nymphs raised their cry. On that day were sown the seeds of suffering and death. Henceforward Dido cared no more for appearances or her good name, and ceased to take any thought for secrecy in her love. She called it a marriage; she used this word to screen her sin.

At once Rumour raced through Africa's great cities. Rumour is of all pests the swiftest. In her freedom of movement lies her power, and she gathers new strength from her going. She begins as a small and timorous creature; but then she grows till she towers into the air, and though she walks on the ground, she hides her head in the clouds. Men say that Earth, Mother of All, brought her to birth when provoked to anger against the gods; she is her last child, younger sister to Coeus and Enceladus. Rumour is fleet of foot, and swift are her wings; she is a vast, fearful monster, with a watchful eye miraculously set under every feather which grows on her, and for every one of them a tongue in a mouth which is loud of speech, and an ear ever alert. By night she flies hissing through the dark in the space between earth and sky, and never droops her eyelids in contented sleep. In the daylight she keeps watch, sometimes perched on the roof-top of a house and sometimes on the tall towers of a palace. And she strikes dread throughout great cities, for she is as retentive of news which is false and wicked as she is ready to tell what is true.

Now, in great joy, she spread various talk among the peoples of Africa, repeating alike facts and fictions; how there had arrived one Aeneas, descended from the blood of Troy, and how the beautiful Dido had deigned to unite herself to him; and how they were now spending all the long winter together in comfort and self-indulgence, caught in the snare of shameful passion, with never a thought of their royal duty. Such was the talk which this foul goddess everywhere inserted into the conversations of men. Next she turned her quick steps towards King Iarbas, spoke to him, set his thoughts on fire, and heaped fuel on his fury.

Jupiter Ammon had ravished an African nymph and Iarbas was his son by her. To this Jupiter he had erected a hundred vast temples and a hundred altars about his broad realm; he had consecrated in them wakeful temple-fires and courses of priests to keep unbroken vigils for the gods. The precincts reeked always with blood of sacrifice, and the temple-gates were ever decked with flowers of many hues. It is said that Iarbas, bitterly angry at what he now heard, and frantic in his helplessness, stood before an altar with the divine presences about him, raised hands in supplication, and prayed long prayers to Jupiter: 'O Jupiter Almighty, to whom now the Moorish nation, banqueting on divans of rich-coloured weave, pours Bacchic offering in your honour, do you see what is done? Or, when you cast your spinning thunderbolt, Father, is our dread of you vain? Are those fires which affright us in the clouds blind fires, and is there no meaning behind their mingled and muttering growl? For a woman, a vagrant, who has built a small city on my territory, renting a coastal strip to cultivate under conditions of tenure dictated by me, has rejected my marriage-suit, and accepted Aeneas as her master and joint ruler. So now this second Paris, wearing a Phrygian bonnet to tie up his chin and cover his oily hair, and attended by a train of she-men, is to become the owner of what he has stolen. Meanwhile, here I am bringing my offerings to temples which I take to be yours, though apparently the belief on which I act is quite mistaken.'

Such were the words of his prayer, and as he prayed he touched the altar. The Almighty heard, and turned his eyes on the queen's city and on these lovers who had forgotten their nobler fame. He then spoke to Mercury, and entrusted him with this commission: 'Up, son of mine, go on your way. Call to you the western winds. Glide on your wings! Speak to the

Dardan prince who is now lingering in Tyrian Carthage with never a thought for those other cities which are his by destiny. Go swiftly through the air and take my words to him. It was never for this that the most beautiful goddess, his mother, twice rescued him from his Greek foes. This is not the man she led us to think that he would prove to be. No, he was to guide an Italy which is to be a breeding-ground of leadership and clamorous with noise of war, transmit a lineage from proud Teucer's blood, and subject the whole earth to the rule of law. And even if the glory of this great destiny is powerless to kindle his ardour, and if he will exert no effort to win fame for himself, will he withhold from his son Ascanius the Fortress of Rome? What does he mean to do? What can he gain by lingering among a people who are his foes, without a care for his own descendants, the Italians of the future, and for the lands destined to bear Lavinia's name? He must set sail. That is what I have to say, and that is to be my message to him.'

He finished, and Mercury prepared to obey his exalted Father's command. First he laced on his feet those golden sandals with wings to carry him high at the speed of the winds' swift blast over ocean and over land alike. Then he took his wand; the wand with which he calls the pale souls forth from the Nether World and sends others down to grim Tartarus, gives sleep, and takes sleep away, and unseals eyes at death. So shepherding the winds before him with his wand, he swam through the murk of the clouds. And now as he flew he discerned the crest and steep flanks of Atlas the enduring, who supports the sky upon his head. His pine-clad crown is perpetually girt by blackest mist and beaten by wind and rain, his shoulders swathed in a mantle of snow, his aged chin a cascade of torrents, and his wild and shaggy beard frozen stiff with ice. Here Cyllenian Mercury first stopped, poised on balancing wings. And from here he plunged with all his weight to the waves; like a sea-bird flying low close to the sea's surface round shores and rocks where fish are found. So did the Cyllenian fly between earth and sky to the sandy shore of Africa, cutting through the winds from the Mountain Atlas, his mother's sire.

As soon as his winged feet had carried him as far as the hut-villages of Africa, he saw Aeneas engaged on the foundations of the citadel and the construction of new dwellings. He had a sword starred with golden-brown jasper, and wore a cloak of bright Tyrian purple draped from his shoulders, a present from a wealthy giver, Dido herself, who had made it, picking out the warp-thread with a line of gold. Mercury immediately delivered his message: 'What, are you siting foundations for proud Carthage and building here a noble city? A model husband! For shame! You forget your destiny and that other kingdom which is to be yours. He who reigns over all the gods, he who sways all the earth and the sky by the power of his will, has himself sent me down to you from glittering Olympus. It is he who commanded me to carry this message to you swiftly through the air. What do you mean to do? What can you gain by living at wasteful leisure in African lands? If the glory of your great destiny is

powerless to kindle your ardour, and if you will exert
no effort to win fame for yourself, at least think of
Ascanius, now growing up, and all that you hope from
him as your heir, destined to rule in an Italy which shall
become the Italy of Rome.' With this stern rebuke, and
even while he was still speaking, Mercury vanished
from mortal vision and melted from sight into thin air.

Aeneas was struck dumb by the vision. He was out
of his wits, his hair bristled with a shiver of fear, and
his voice was checked in his throat. Already he was
ardently wishing to flee from the land of his love and be
gone; so violent had been the shock of this peremptory
warning from the gods. But what could he do? How
could he dare to speak to the infatuated queen, and
win her round? What would be the best opening for
him to choose? Rapidly he turned it over in his mind,
inclining now to one plan and now to another, and
hurriedly considering all the different aspects and
possibilities. As he pondered, one policy seemed pre-
ferable to every other. He called to him Mnestheus,
Sergestus, and the gallant Serestus: they were to fit out
the fleet, make ready all their tackle, and muster their
comrades on the shore, without giving any expla-
nations, and concealing the reason for the change of
plan. Meanwhile he would see Dido, for in her ignor-
ance and goodness of heart she would never suspect
that so deep a love could possibly be broken. So he
would try to find the right approach and the least
painful moment to speak, and discover a tactful way
out of their predicament.

His men obeyed with pleasure and alacrity and be-

gan carrying out their orders. But no one can deceive
a lover. The queen divined the intended deceit in
advance. Before she was told, her intuition discerned
what would happen and her fears were alive to every
possible danger, real or unreal. In this nervous state the
news came to her, brought, once more, by unholy
Rumour, that the fleet was being equipped in pre-
paration for a voyage. Furious, and quite unable to face
the truth, she ran in excited riot about Carthage, like
a Bacchanal uplifted to frenzy as the emblems of
Bacchus are shaken and the cry of his name is heard,
when every second year the thrill of the festival pricks
her and Mount Cithaeron calls her with shouting in
the night. At last Dido accosted Aeneas, speaking first,
and denounced him:

'Traitor, did you actually believe that you could dis-
guise so wicked a deed and leave my country without
a word? And can nothing hold you, not our love, nor
our once plighted hands, nor even the cruel death that
must await your Dido? Are you so unfeeling that you
labour at your fleet under a wintry sky, in haste to
traverse the high seas in the teeth of the northerly
gales? Why, had you not now been searching for a
home which you have never seen in some alien land,
and had ancient Troy itself been still standing, would
you have been planning to sail even there over such
tempestuous seas? Is it from me that you are trying to
escape? Oh, by the tears which I shed, by your own
plighted hand, for I have left myself, poor fool, no
other appeal, and by our union, by the true marriage
which it was to be, oh, if I was ever kind to you, or if

anything about me made you happy, please, please, if it is not too late to beg you, have pity for the ruin of a home, and change your mind. It was because of you that I earned the hate of Africa's tribes and the lords of the Numidians, and the hostility of my own Tyrians also; and it was because of you that I let my honour die, the fair fame which used to be mine, and my only hope of immortality. In whose hands are you leaving me to face my death, my – Guest? I used to call you Husband, but the word has shrunk to Guest. What does the future hold for me now? My brother Pygmalion coming to demolish my walls, or this Gaetulian Iarbas, marrying me by capture? At least, if I had a son of yours conceived before you left, some tiny Aeneas to play about my hall and bring you back to me if only in his likeness, I might not then have felt so utterly entrapped and forsaken.'

She finished. He, remembering Jupiter's warning, held his eyes steady, and strained to master the agony within him. At last he spoke, shortly: 'Your Majesty, I shall never deny that I am in your debt for all those many acts of kindness which you may well recount to me. And for as long as I have consciousness and breath of life controls my movement, I shall never tire, Elissa, of your memory. Now I shall speak briefly of the facts. I had no thought of hiding my present departure under any deceit. Do not imagine that. Nor have I ever made any marriage-rite my pretext, for I never had such a compact with you. If my destiny had allowed me to guide my life as I myself would have chosen, and solve my problems according to my own preference, I should

have made the city of Troy, with its loved remem-
brances of my own folk, my first care; and, with Priam's
tall citadel still standing, I should have refounded
Troy's fortress to be strong once more after her defeat.
But in fact Apollo at Grynium, where he gives his
divination in Lycia by the lots, has insistently com-
manded me to make my way to Italy's noble land. Italy
must be my love and my homeland now. If you, a
Phoenician, are faithful to your Carthaginian fortress
here, content to look on no other city but this city in
far-away Africa, what is the objection if Trojans settle
in Italy? It is no sin, if we, like you, look for a kingdom
in a foreign country. Each time the night shrouds the
earth in its moist shadows, each time the fiery stars
arise, the anxious wraith of my father Anchises warns
me in sleep, and I am afraid. My son Ascanius also
serves as a warning to me; I think of his dear self, and
of the wrong which I do him in defrauding him of his
Italian kingdom, where Fate has given him his lands.
And now Jove himself has sent the Spokesman of the
Gods – this I swear to you by my son's life and by my
father – who flew swiftly through the air, and delivered
the command to me. With my own eyes I saw the
divine messenger in clearest light entering the city gate,
and heard his voice with my own ears. Cease, therefore,
to upset yourself, and me also, with these protests. It
is not by my own choice that I voyage onward to Italy.'

Throughout this declaration Dido had remained
standing, turned away from Aeneas but glaring at him
over her shoulder with eyes which roved about his
whole figure in a voiceless stare. Then her fury broke:

'Traitor, no goddess was ever your mother, nor was it Dardanus who founded your line. No, your parent was Mount Caucasus, rugged, rocky, and hard, and tigers of Hyrcania nursed you ... For what need have I of concealment now? Why hold myself in check any longer, as if there could be anything worse to come? ... Has he spared a sigh or a look in response to my weeping, or has he once softened, or shed a tear of pity for one who loved him? Depth beyond depth of iniquity! Neither Supreme Juno, nor the Father who is Saturn's son, can possibly look with the impartial eyes of justice on what is happening now. No faith is left sure in the wide world. I welcomed him, a shipwrecked beggar, and like a fool I allowed him to share my royal place. I saved his comrades from death and gave him back his lost fleet ... The Furies have me now, they burn, they drive ... ! So, now, it seems, he has his orders from Apollo's own Lycian oracle, and next even the Spokesman of the Gods is sent by Jove himself to deliver through the air to him the same ghastly command! So I am to believe that the High Powers exercise their minds about such a matter and let concern for it disturb their calm! Oh, I am not holding you. I do not dispute your words. Go, quest for Italy before the winds; sail over the waves in search of your kingdom. But I still believe that, if there is any power for righteousness in Heaven, you will drink to the dregs the cup of punishment amid sea-rocks, and as you suffer cry "Dido" again and again. Though far, yet I shall be near, haunting you with flames of blackest pitch. And when death's chill has parted my body from its breath, wherever you go my spectre will be there. You will have your punishment, you villain. And I shall hear; the news will reach me deep in the world of death.' She did not finish, but at these words broke off sharply. She hurried in her misery away and hid from sight, leaving Aeneas anxious and hesitant, and longing to say much more to her. Dido fainted, and fell; and her maids took her up, carried her to her marble bedroom, and laid her on her bed.

Meanwhile Aeneas the True longed to allay her grief and dispel her sufferings with kind words. Yet he remained obedient to the divine command, and with many a sigh, for he was shaken to the depths by the strength of his love, returned to his ships. Vigorously indeed the Trojans set to work. They were soon launching their tall galleys all along the beach, and the freshly tarred keels were again afloat. Men carried rough oars with the leaves still on them, and tough timbers as yet unworked, from the forest, so keen were they to be gone. They could all be seen on the move hurrying from every quarter of the city, looking like ants, which, planning for the winter ahead, pillage some large heap of barley for storing in their homes, and march in a long black line across a plain, conveying their plunder on a narrow trail over the grass; some press shoulders against a massive grain of corn, forcing it onwards; others bring up the rear and punish stragglers; and the whole track is a ferment of activity. What must have been Dido's thoughts when she saw all this movement, and how bitterly must she have sighed as she looked from her commanding citadel, and discerned the lively bustle along the shore and all the turmoil of loud confusion on the sea? Ah, merciless Love, is there any length to which you cannot force the human heart to go? For Love now drove Dido to have recourse to tears again, and again to try what entreaties might do, subjecting pride to passion in a last appeal, in case she had still left some way unexplored, and was going to a needless death.

'Anna,' she said, 'you see the hurrying all over the beach. From all sides they have gathered there. Already their canvas invites the wind, and the mariners have been gaily setting garlands on the sterns of their ships. Perhaps I might have foreseen this terrible grief. Perhaps too, Anna, I shall have strength to endure it. But nevertheless do carry out this one task for your poor sister. For that traitor was never really attentive to anyone but you; you alone had his full confidence, and only you ever knew just how and when to approach this hard man tactfully. So go now, sister, and speak in humble appeal to our haughty enemy. I am not one who conspired with the Greeks at Aulis to exterminate the Trojan people – I sent no fleet against the fortress of Troy – I never tore up Anchises' grave to disturb his ashes and his spirit. So why should his pitiless ears refuse to listen to my plea? And where is he going in such haste? As one last gift to his unhappy love, he might at least make his own flight easier simply by awaiting a favourable wind. I do not now beg him to restore our honoured marriage as it was before he betrayed it, or ask him to forgo his splendid Latium where he hopes to reign. I ask only the time of inaction, to give my mad mood a breathing-space and a rest, until my fortune can teach me submission and the art of grief. This is my last plea for indulgence, and you must bear with me as a sister. And when he has granted it to me I shall repay the debt, with the interest, in death.'

Such was Dido's entreaty; and her poor, unhappy sister carried the tearful messages between them. But all these appeals left Aeneas quite unmoved. He was deaf to every plea, for destiny barred the way and a divine influence checked his inclination to listen kindly. He stood firm like a strong oak-tree toughened by the years when northern winds from the Alps vie together to tear it from the soil, with their blasts striking on it now this side and now that; creaking, the trunk shakes, and leaves from on high strew the ground; yet still the tree grips among the rocks below, for its roots stretch as far down towards the abyss as its crest reaches up to airs of heaven. Like that tree, the hero was battered this side and that by their insistent pleas, and deeply his brave heart grieved. But his will remained unshaken. The tears rolled down, but without effect.

It was final. Dido was lost; and she saw with horror the fate starkly confronting her. Her one prayer was now for death. The sight of heaven's vault was only weariness to her. And, as if to steel her will to fulfil her design and to part from the light of day, as she laid her offerings on the altars where incense burned, she saw a dreadful sight; for the holy waters turned to black and the poured wine by some sinister transformation was changed into blood. She told no one, not even her sister, what she had seen. And furthermore there was in her palace a marble chapel, sacred to her first husband, which she venerated with utmost love, keeping it decorated with snowy fleeces and festal greenery. Now from this chapel when night held the world in darkness she thought that she distinctly heard cries, as of her husband calling to her. And often on a rooftop a lonely owl would sound her deathly lamentation, drawing out her notes into a long wail. Then many presages of ancient seers shocked her to panic by their dread warnings. She would have nightmares of a furious Aeneas pursuing her, and driving her wild with fear, and of being left utterly alone, and travelling companionless a long road, searching for Tyrian friends in a deserted land. She was in the state of Pentheus, when, with mind deranged, he saw the Furies advancing in ranks, two suns appearing in the sky, and two cities of Thebes; or of Agamemnon's tormented son Orestes on the theatre-stage, seeking to escape a mother armed with firebrands and black snakes, while the avenging Spirits of the Curse wait at the door.

So agony prevailed; and Dido was possessed by demon-powers. Having made her decision for death, she first worked out, all by herself, the time and the means. Then, with a calm and hopeful expression to conceal her plan, she accosted her distressed sister and spoke to her: 'Sister, Anna, congratulate me! For I have found the way which will either give him back to me or release me from loving him. Close to Ocean's margin and the setting of the sun lies the land of Aethiopia on the edge of the world, where giant Atlas holds, turning, on his shoulders the pole of the heavens, inset with blazing stars. I have been told of a Massylian priestess living in that land. She guards the Temple of the Hesperides; it was she who fed the dragon, sprinkling honey-drops and poppy-seed, bringer of sleep, and it was she who kept watch over the holy boughs on the tree. She professes by her spells to give freedom to the hearts of any whom she chooses, but to inflict cruel agonies on others. She can stay the current of a river, and reverse the movement of stars. She can evoke the spirits in the night-time; yes, and as you will see, make the earth bellow underfoot, and the rowan-trees march down from their hills. Dear Anna, I swear to you by the gods, I swear by you and your own sweet life that it is against my will that I arm myself with magic. Now, build me a tall funeral pyre. Build it in the centre of our home under the open sky but out of view. Lay on it the arms of the false man, which he left hanging from a wall in our bridal room, and all the garments which he wore, besides; and you must also place on it the bridal bed which was my ruin. I choose to destroy whatever can remind me of one who must never be mentioned. Besides, such is the advice of the priestess.' After saying this she fell silent, and her face suddenly paled. It never occurred to Anna that her sister was using this strange rite to veil her own impending death. She could not herself imagine so violent a passion, and had no fear of anything worse happening now than had happened when Sychaeus died. So she made the preparations, as Dido had asked.

Presently the pyre had been built with logs of

holm-oak and pine. It was vast, rising to a great height, and it stood in the centre of the building. The queen had festooned the hall with flower-chains, and wreathed the pyre with the greenery of death. On it was the bed, and there she placed a sword which Aeneas had left, with garments which he had worn, and a portrait of him, knowing all the time what was to be. Around it were altars. The priestess, hair astream, told in a voice like thunder the names of her thrice-hundred gods, told Erebos and the Void, and Hecate of three forms, who is Diana the maiden of the triple countenance. She had sprinkled water, supposed to be from the fount of Avernus. Herbs, reaped with bronzen sickles by moonlight and bursting with a black poisonous milk, were gathered there, and with them a love-charm ripped from the brow of a baby foal before the mother could take it. Close to the high altar stood Dido, holding the sacred meal and lifting pure hands above, with garment girt back and one foot unsandalled. And, soon to die, she called on the gods and the stars which know fate's secrets to hear her. And she added a prayer to any Power there may be, some Power watchful and fair, with a thought for lovers whose love is not matched well.

It was night, and tired creatures all over the world were enjoying kindly sleep. Forests and fierce seas were at rest, as the circling constellations glided in their midnight course. Every field, all the farm-animals, and the colourful birds were silent, all that lived across miles of glassy mere and in the wild country's ragged brakes, lying still under the quiet night in a sleep which smoothed each care away from hearts which had forgotten life's toil. But not so the Phoenician queen. Her accursed spirit could not relax into sleeping, or welcome darkness into her eyes or brain. Instead, her torment redoubled; her love came back again and again, and heaved in ocean-tides of rage. And she began yet once more to pursue her thoughts, communing with herself in her heart: 'There! What is there for me to do? Risk mockery by returning to my former suitors, sound their feelings, and plead humbly with some Numidian to marry me, though time after time I have scorned to think of one of them as a husband? Or instead should I sail with the Trojan fleet and submit to Trojan orders however harsh? Am I so sure that they are pleased with the aid and relief which I gave them, that they remember, and that their gratefulness for what I did then is still alive? But indeed, even granted that I wished it, would they let me come, and welcome me to their ships? They are arrogant, and hate me. Lost fool, can you not see? Can you even now not realize how treacherous Laomedon's nation can be? Besides, if I sail with these mariners, who are so triumphant now at their departure, do I go alone, or do I take with me all my Tyrian friends, thronging round me when I go to join the Trojans? If so, how can I order them to spread their sails to the winds and force them to voyage once more out onto the ocean? It was all that I could do to uproot them from their former city, Sidon. No. You have deserved death and you must die. Only the blade can save you from the agony . . . O Anna, I have been mad; but it was you who first laid on me this load of suffering, for you gave way to my tears, and set me at the mercy of my foe. If only I could have been allowed to pass my life free from reproach as the wild animals do, without any wedding, and in no danger of anguish like mine . . . And the vow which I made to the ashes of Sychaeus is broken too.' Such were the terrible words of grief which burst from Dido's heart.

Meanwhile Aeneas, who had now settled his plans for sailing and completed his preparations, was lying asleep on his ship's stern. As he slept he again had a vision of the god, who returned in countenance as before and was like Mercury in every feature, in his voice and complexion, his blond hair, and limbs with the grace of youth. As Aeneas gazed, Mercury repeated his warning: 'Son of the Goddess, can you, with so great a disaster impending, remain asleep, and not discern the dangers which wait ready to break about your head? Fool! Can you not hear the breath of the favouring west winds? She plans in her thought a fearful and treacherous wrong. In her a violent rage surges and surges again, and she is resolved to die. Will you not hasten away while it is not too late for hastening? You will soon see a confusion of wreckage on the sea, the cruel glare of firebrands burning bright, and the whole shore ablaze, if dawn finds you still lingering here. Ho! Come, have done with delays. Women were ever things of many changing moods.' So he spoke, and then melted into the black darkness.

Aeneas was shocked indeed by the sudden apparition. He leapt up and gave his comrades the alarm:

'Hasten, men! Awake! Take your places for rowing. Quick, unfurl your sails! For, see! Again a god has descended from high heaven, and again he stings us into haste. We must hack through our twisted hawsers, and flee. We follow you, holy Deity, whoever you may truly be, and we joyfully obey your command, as before. Be with us and graciously aid us. Bring us favours from the stars of heaven.' With the words he quickly unsheathed his sword and struck the cables with the flashing blade. One ardour seized them all. They heaved and they hurried. Not one remained on shore. The water was hidden beneath the fleet. They bent to it, churned the foam, and swept the blue surface of the sea.

By now Aurora, rising, had left the saffron bed of Tithonus and was sprinkling her fresh light on the world. From her watch-tower the queen saw the white gleam of dawn, and saw the fleet moving forward with sails square to the wind. She realized that the shore and the harbour were empty, without a single oarsman. At the sight, she struck her beautiful breast, three times struck it and then a fourth, she tore her golden hair, and she cried aloud: 'Ah, Jupiter! Is this stranger to make a mock of my realm, and calmly go? Fetch weapons! Come on, every one in Carthage! Pursue! You there, rush to the dockyards and launch your ships! Quick! Bring some fire-brands, hand out arms. Put your weight to the oars! ... Oh, what am I saying? Where am I? Oh, poor, poor Dido, what mad folly is distorting your mind? Is it only now that his wicked deeds strike home to you? Why did you not think of that before you relinquished to him your sovereignty? See his faithfulness to his plighted word! And yet they say that he carries with him the gods of his ancestral home, and bowed his shoulders to bear his old and feeble father! Could I not have seized him, torn him limb from limb, and scattered the pieces on the waves? And put his comrades to the sword – yes, and killed Ascanius and served him up to be his father's meal? Ah, but the fortune of such a fight was never certain. Uncertain, then. But whom had I to fear, having, in any event, to die? I might have taken firebrands into their camp and set all their ships' decks blazing. I could have quenched the life of son, of father, and of all their line. And then, to crown all, I could have flung myself to death. Sun, whose cleansing beams survey the whole world and all its works! Juno, who share with me the secret of my agony and could tell its truth! Hecate, honoured at every city's three-cross-ways by wavering holloas in the night! Terrible Spirits of Avenging Curse! Angels of Death awaiting Elissa! All of you, hear me now. Direct the force of your divine will, as you must, on the evil here, and listen to my prayer. If that wicked being must sail surely to land and come to harbour, because such is the fixed and destined ending required by Jupiter's own ordinances, yet let him afterwards suffer affliction in war through the arms of a daring foe, let him be banished from his own territory, and torn from the embraces of Iulus, imploring aid as he sees his innocent friends die, and then, after surrendering to a humiliating peace, may he not live to enjoy his kingdom in days of happiness; but may he lie fallen before his time, unburied on a lonely strand. That is my prayer and my last cry, and it comes from me with my life-blood streaming. From then onwards shall you, my Phoenicians, torment with acts of pursuing hate all his descendants to come, each member of his line. This service shall be your offering to my shade. Neither love nor compact shall there be between the nations. And from my dead bones may some Avenger arise to persecute with fire and sword those settlers from Troy, soon or in after-time, whenever the strength is given! Let your shores oppose their shores, your waves their waves, your arms their arms. That is my imprecation. Let them fight, they, and their sons' sons, for ever!'

Such was her curse. And now she turned to consider every course of action, for she wanted, as quickly as might be, to break off her living in day's hated light. She spoke shortly to Barce, who had been Sychaeus' old nurse – her own nurse, dark ashes now, had been left in the ancient homeland – : 'Nurse, dear, ask Anna my sister to come to me here. And tell her she should hasten to sprinkle river-water over her, and bring with her the victims and all else that is needed for the atonement which I have been commanded to make. Let her come, prepared as I say; and you yourself should wreathe your brow with a ribbon of piety. It is my intention to complete certain rites to Stygian Jupiter, which I have formally prepared and begun, and to put an end to my sorrow by committing to the flames the pyre which holds the Trojan's life.' So she spoke. Barce, with all an old woman's interest, quickened her pace.

But Dido, in trembling haste and frantic at her desperate design, burst through the doorway into the inner room. Her eyes were reddened and rolling, her cheeks quivered under a flush, and she was pale with the pallor of imminent death. In a mad dash she climbed the high funeral pile, and unsheathed the Trojan sword, a gift never meant for such a use as this. Her sight rested on the garments which had come from Troy, and on the bed with its memories. She paused a little for tears and for a thought; and she cast herself down on the bed, and there spoke her last words: 'Sweet relics, sweet so long as God and Destiny allowed, now receive my life-breath, and set me free from this suffering. I have lived my life and finished the course which Fortune allotted me. Now my wraith shall pass in state to the world below. I have established a noble city. I have lived to see my own ramparts built. I have avenged my husband and punished the brother who was our foe. Happy, all too happy, should I have been, if only the Dardan ships had never reached my coast!' With this cry she buried her face in the bed, and continued: 'I shall die, and die unavenged; but die I shall. Yes, yes; this is the way I like to go into the dark. And may the heartless Trojan, far out on the deep, drink in the sight of my fire and take with him the evil omen of my death.'

There she ended. And even while she still spoke she had fallen upon the blade. Soon her attendants saw her with blood foaming about the sword and the stains of it on her hands. A cry rose to the palace-roof. Carthage was striken by the shock and Rumour ran riot in the town. Lamentation and sobbing and women's wailing rang through the houses, and high heaven echoed with the loud mourning; as if some enemy had broken through and all Carthage, or ancient Tyre, were falling, with the flames rolling madly up over dwellings of gods and men. Her sister heard, and the breath left her. Marring her cheeks with her finger-nails and bruising her breast with her clenched hands, she dashed in frightened haste through the crowds, found Dido at the very point of death, and cried out to her: 'O Sister, so this was the truth? You planned to deceive me! Was this what your pyre, your altars, and the fires were to mean for me? How shall I begin reproaching you for forsaking me so? Did you scorn your own sister and not want her with you when you died? You should have asked me to share your fate, and then one same hour, one agony of the blade, might have taken us both. To think that with my own hands I even built the pyre, and cried loud upon our ancestral gods, only to be cruelly separated from you as you lay in death! Sister, you have destroyed my life with your own, and the lives of our people and Sidon's nobility, and your whole city too. Come, let me see your wounds – I must wash them clean with water, and gather with my own lips any last hovering breath.' While speaking she had climbed to the top of the steps and clasped her sister, who was still just breathing, to her breast, and fondled her, sobbing, and trying to stanch the dark blood with her dress. Dido attempted to raise her heavy eyes again, but failed; and the deep wound in her breast, where the sword stood planted, breathed loud. Three times she rose, supporting herself on her elbows, but each time she rolled back onto the bed. With roaming eyes she looked to high heaven for the daylight, and found it, and gave a sigh.

But Juno who has all power took pity on the long anguish of her difficult death, and sent Iris down from Olympus to release the wrestling spirit from the twined limbs. For since she perished neither by destiny nor by a death deserved, but tragically, before her day, in the mad heat of a sudden passion, Proserpine had not yet taken a golden lock from her head, to assign her life to Stygian Orcus. So therefore Iris, saffron-winged, sparkling like dew and trailing a thousand colours as she caught the light of the sun, flew down across the sky. She hovered over Dido's head: 'By command I take this lock as an offering to Pluto; and I release you from the body which was yours.' Speaking so, she held out a hand and cut the lock. At once, all the warmth fell away, and the life passed into the moving air.

THE STORY OF PENGUIN CLASSICS

Before 1946 ...'Classics' are mainly the domain of academics and students, without readable editions for everyone else. This all changes when a little-known classicist, E. V. Rieu, presents Penguin founder Allen Lane with the translation of Homer's Odyssey that he has been working on and reading to his wife Nelly in his spare time.

1946 The Odyssey becomes the first Penguin Classic published, and promptly sells three million copies. Suddenly, classic books are no longer for the privileged few.

1950s Rieu, now series editor, turns to professional writers for the best modern, readable translations, including Dorothy L. Sayers's *Inferno* and Robert Graves's *The Twelve Caesars*, which revives the salacious original.

1960s 1961 sees the arrival of the Penguin Modern Classics, showcasing the best twentieth-century writers from around the world. Rieu retires in 1964, hailing the Penguin Classics list as 'the greatest educative force of the 20th century'.

1970s A new generation of translators arrives to swell the Penguin Classics ranks, and the list grows to encompass more philosophy, religion, science, history and politics.

1980s The Penguin American Library joins the Classics stable, with titles such as *The Last of the Mohicans* safeguarded. Penguin Classics now offers the most comprehensive library of world literature available.

1990s Penguin Popular Classics are launched, offering readers budget editions of the greatest works of literature. Penguin Audiobooks brings the classics to a listening audience for the first time, and in 1999 the launch of the Penguin Classics website takes them online to an ever larger global readership.

The 21st Century Penguin Classics are rejacketed for the first time in nearly twenty years. This world famous series now consists of more than 1,300 titles, making the widest range of the best books ever written available to millions – and constantly redefining the meaning of what makes a 'classic'.

The Odyssey continues ...

The best books ever written

PENGUIN CLASSICS

SINCE 1946